LARGE PRINT

RIMROCK

G·K Hall &Co.

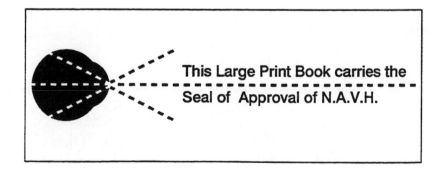

This Large Print Book carries the
Seal of Approval of N.A.V.H.

RIMROCK

Luke Short

G.K. Hall & Co.
Thorndike, Maine

Published in 1996 by arrangement with
Kate Hirson and Daniel Glidden.

G.K. Hall Large Print Western Collection.

The text of this Large Print edition is unabridged.
Other aspects of the book may vary from the original edition.

Set in 16 pt. News Plantin by Rick Gundberg.

Printed in the United States on permanent paper.

Library of Congress Cataloging in Publication Data

Short, Luke, 1908–1975.
  Rimrock / Luke Short.
    p.   cm.
  ISBN 0-7838-1465-8 (lg. print : hc)
  1. Large type books. I. Title.
  [PS3513.L68158R55 1996]
  813'.54—dc20   95-24419

RIMROCK

1

When Dave Borthen walked into the lighted lobby of the old hotel, Bowie Sutton, the elevator operator, was the first to spot him. Smiling, Bowie rose, took his bag and sample case and said, "Welcome home, Borthen. Have a nice vacation?"

"Thanks, Bowie. It was way too short." He gave the old man's arm an affectionate squeeze, then crossed the ancient lobby to the scrollwork desk and asked for his mail. The clerk, new since he'd been gone, took a bundle of letters from the rack behind him and Dave accepted them and was heading for the elevator when the clerk called, "Oh, Mr. Borthen! One of our guests wanted you to call him as soon as you got in."

Dave halted. "What name?"

"A Mr. Clyde Elliott."

Dave wondered if the irritation showed on his face, but he only asked idly, "How long has he been here?"

"Two days."

"Okay, get him on the phone," Dave said, and he cut over to the house phone behind the elevator. He was a tall young man, hatless, and his short crew haircut could not destroy entirely the tight curl in his chestnut hair. Even the most obtuse hotel clerk, by noting the double-breasted suit, the inevitable white shirt and the carefully shined shoes, could have identified him as a salesman. His long angular face would have been handsome except that his nose was a little crooked and his ears faintly bat-winged. His eyes were blue and deep-set under heavy brows.

As he palmed up the phone, a fleeting look of worry touched his tanned face, and then his voice came firmly, the voice of the salesman, as he said, "Clyde? Dave. I just got in. What are you doing out here in the back brush?"

"Just making the rounds, boy, just making the rounds. That and another matter. About a certain letter you wrote me." His voice, Dave noted, was equally hearty, but to an experienced ear it contained a note of injured ego.

"That letter said everything I've got to say, Clyde."

"I don't believe it for a minute. Why don't you come up?"

Dave hesitated, then said, "Be right with you."

He moved to the pay telephone, dialed a number and when he got it, smiled. "Hi, Abby!"

"I got your telegram, Dave. Hurry on over."

"Put the borsch on the back of the stove, doll, I'm being delayed."

"Now what?" Abby's voice was calm, as he knew it would be.

"Our sales manager is in town. He's been here two days shredding his fingernails, waiting for me."

"Didn't he know you were on vacation?"

8

"He forgets easy," Dave said grimly.

"Well, happy landing. Will you come over later?"

"Yeah. Probably in a basket. Good-bye, now." Afterwards, with Bowie promising to deliver his bags, Dave left the elevator at the fourth floor and turned left. The next hour, he knew, was apt to be a rugged one.

Taking a deep breath, he moved across to 403, knocked firmly and stepped inside. Clyde Elliott, western sales manager of Silver Plume Asphalt Tile, shed a harried look as he rose from a bed strewn with neatly piled correspondence. Although white-haired, he was in his middle fifties, trim of figure, wan of complexion, and his wallpaper tie upon a spotless white shirt held the same neat knot that had been tied into it at nine that morning. A practiced affability took over the controls as he rose, smiled, and warmly shook Dave's hand. "You're a hard lad to follow, Dave."

"If I am on vacation, that's the way I want it, Clyde."

Elliott laughed without humor. "Like a drink?"

When Dave said yes, Elliott turned to the desk where ice and glasses were waiting on the tray. Dave, with the salesman's habit, hunted up a straight-back chair upon which to hang his coat, and then seated himself, a wariness touching him.

Elliott gave him his drink, then sank down on the bed, and Dave waited for the small talk to begin. At Elliott's first words, however, Dave knew it would be no small talk.

9

"About your letter of resignation, Dave. It's been rejected by Silver Plume."

"You're a miracle man, Clyde, but even you can't reject a letter of resignation."

"What are you unhappy about? Whatever it is, we can fix it."

"I'm not unhappy. I just quit."

"But why?" Elliott asked sharply. "Let's be candid, Dave."

"All right, I'm just going into business on my own."

"What business?"

"My affair, Clyde."

They looked at each other carefully. Then Elliott asked in injured tone, "You think that's fair, Dave? Here Silver Plume hired you, trained you and now that we've barely got back our investment in you, you quit."

"That's right," Dave said in perfect agreement.

"And you won't tell us why you're leaving us."

"Right again."

"I'll tell you why," Elliott said. "You're going uranium-prospecting in Utah."

Dave asked dryly, "Where'd you get that notion?"

"From your girl."

"I doubt that."

"What?"

"I'll put it politely. I don't believe you."

Elliott hunched even farther forward on the bed, his drink forgotten. "Remember, I've been around here two days waiting for you. I did a little asking around. It's fairly common knowledge in this rube town that the subject of uranium fascinates you. Knowing that much, I called your girl. I told her I was a college friend of yours, a mining engineer just passing through. I said I was going up to Utah to look over some uranium property and that I wanted some advice. She came through beautifully."

"So now you know," Dave said.

Undisguised outrage came to Elliott's face. "You're throwing over your whole future! You're acting like a damned kid, Dave! You'll go batting off in the desert when J.B. would give you any job in the home office you named."

"You couldn't have put it more beautifully."

"You even planned to be on vacation when J.B. got your letter, didn't you?"

Dave took a sip of his drink and nodded. "I figured you and J.B. would be hacking at me morning, noon and night. You tried to, didn't you?"

"But we've got an investment in you." His tone of voice was terribly earnest now. "Come back, Dave, and you can write your own ticket. J.B. will be reasonable. I know he will, because when I left he said, 'I'll be reasonable, Clyde. Just get him back.'"

"J.B. can be as reasonable as he wants, but not with me." Dave leaned forward now and said, "Look, get off your knees, Clyde. Silver Plume has been good to me and I've been good to it, but the marriage was never meant to last. You've earned your ulcer. Now go back and tell J.B. my

11

mind's made up. Tell him I'm on my own."

"He'll never take you back if I do!" Elliott said angrily.

Dave stood up and said, "I hope that's a promise, Clyde." He shrugged into his coat, moved toward the door, then halted and picked up the bottle of whiskey on the table and read its label. Looking at Elliott, he set the bottle down gently and observed, "If J.B. can afford to send you all the way from Omaha, he can afford a bottle of whiskey that doesn't turn your teeth black. Make a note of that."

Elliott grunted. "For a guy who's about to eat steaks from a burro, you're pretty particular."

"The day I eat burro steaks I'll be washing them down with eight-dollar-a-bottle champagne."

"You're a chump, Dave."

"But my own brand of a chump. So long, Clyde."

He took the fire stairs to the floor below and let himself into his corner room at the hotel's rear. As he changed out of his suit and took a shower, he went back over the events of the last month. It was little wonder that Elliott had been unable to find him, for he had seen every customer in his territory. On this trip Silver Plume Asphalt Tile had never been mentioned once, yet Dave had done the selling job of his life. What he had sold was stock in a corporation named Rex Uranium which, with the help of a lawyer, he had formed and incorporated. It was a limited stock company and its only stockholders were his dealers who had been levied monthly assessments for the employment of a geologist, a helper, the purchase of a second-hand jeep, a third-hand Geiger Counter and groceries.

As of tonight then, his break with Silver Plume was final — except for one thing. Abby even now believed he had used his vacation to set up a corporation which he would direct in his spare time away from Silver Plume work. Tonight she would learn what Clyde had already learned, that he and Silver Plume, for better or for worse, were finished with each other.

The Channons lived on a tree-shaded corner in a big three-story house on the main street. And as Dave pulled up in front of the house, he noted that Dr. Channon's car was gone from the drive, so he supposed the old boy was on a call. Punching the doorbell, Dave let himself into the bright lamp-lit living room. Papers were scattered over the deep couch and the phonograph to the side of the cold fireplace was softly playing Gershwin.

"Who's that?" came a cheerful voice from above stairs.

"Me, Mrs. Channon," Dave called. "How are you?"

"Oh, Dave, you're back."

A new voice cut in. "I've got him, Ma. Now go back to bed," and Abby Channon entered from the dining room.

She was just under medium height and was wearing an absurd but wonderful combination of black toreador pants and a plain red-flannel hunting shirt with the sleeves rolled up. Her close-cropped hair was curly and its blackness made her blue eyes seem almost gray. She was not, Dave noted with satisfaction, either fashionably spindle-legged or flat-chested, and the only "boyish" thing about her was a seldom used but talented vocabulary of swear words.

She came across to Dave and kissed him warmly, and then she kissed him again. Holding her, Dave murmured, "I ought to come back from the wars oftener."

"That's a special production." She looked up at him. "I thought you'd need a little cheering up."

She took his hand and led him over to the sofa where they both sat down. "Now what's all this trouble I'm cheering you up about?" she asked.

"Who said it was trouble?" Dave asked.

"Why else does a sales manager come clear out here?"

"Well, this one came out to try to change my mind."

Abby frowned. "About what?"

"About quitting."

"Quitting?" Abby cried. "Quitting Silver Plume? Who said?"

"I did, in a letter to J.B. last month."

"Oh, Dave!" Abby said, almost wailing. "And you never told me?"

"I wanted it all set up first, Abby."

"Then what are you going to do?"

"Run a uranium mining company."

Dave watched her, wondering if the news had really shocked or distressed her. However, she was regarding him with almost distant appraisal. "I might have expected this," she said dryly. "You wanted that job like you want a loose tooth."

Dave felt his face flush.

"I thought you'd get it out of your system while you were on vacation. I thought you were rigging up this uranium company just for kicks."

"Not for kicks — for keeps, doll."

Abby just looked at him. "So now you've got the excuse to quit acting like a sensible man. You can lapse back into boyhood. You can be a rich man's Huck Finn and go exploring — for uranium yet."

The bite in her words made Dave wince and he now read the temper in her eyes. He reached out and took her hand, and she yanked it away from him and stood up. "All right, you unemployed salesman, tell me your plans."

Dave scrubbed his short hair with his hand, ran his palm over his face and said, "You won't like them."

"I know I won't, but see if I can guess what they are," Abby said quietly. "Tomorrow you head out for Utah. Somewhere on the way you'll probably trade your car for a jeep. You'll stock up on canned beans and whiskey. Then you'll hunt up that egghead geologist you're paying and let your beard grow. You'll be recording a lot of useless real estate for a syndicate of lumber dealers. In two months you'll be mooching cigarettes and writing me for a loan so you can pay your share for diamond drilling a deep hole. In another month you'll be writing Clydie and telling him you'll reconsider his proposition." She paused, out of breath. "Ha — Ha."

"Well, listen to this," a voice said from the hall, and they both turned their heads. Dr. Channon, black bag still in hand, stood in the doorway from the kitchen. He was a big rumpled man with an impressive belly, a well-upholstered seat, a wing of thick, grayshot hair that would not stay off his forehead and a broad face that at first sight seemed benign. Closer investigation showed his deep-set, sleepy blue eyes were only a shade removed from the sardonic in expression. He was, Dave knew, an able, lazy man who had never hankered after the big money and the big pressures of a city surgeon; he was, in spite of his bulk, a tireless hunter, an artist with a dry fly and a ferocious poker player.

Dr. Channon gently set his bag on a chair and observed, "Think it's time I broke this up?"

"Oh, Dad, Dave resigned his job!"

Dr. Channon looked at Dave. "Congratulations."

Dave laughed, but Abby did not. "What's he to be congratulated about — acting like a bubblehead schoolboy?"

"There should be a higher goal in life than peddling asphalt tile," Dr. Channon said mildly.

"Like spending your life down a hole in the middle of Utah?" Abby demanded.

"Some people have found it rewarding." Dr.

Channon crossed the room, trailing a faint odor of drugs and ether, and sat down in the deep chair by the fireplace.

"Go on, Dave, tell him what you plan. I dare you," Abby taunted.

Dave glanced sheepishly at Dr. Channon. "Well, our boys are staking forty-four claims this week south of Joash, Utah, if our samples assay as good as we think they will. They look good."

"Hear that, Pa? They think these claims that they haven't got might look good."

"Abby!" Dr. Channon said reprovingly.

"But listen to him," Abby said in exasperation. "He's quit his job with nothing in sight, not even a claim staked."

"It's not that bad," Dave said defensively. "We do have a group of twenty-five claims next to the forty-four we're going to stake. We took over these from a man who was leasing them."

"You going to mine all sixty-nine claims? Is that it?" Abby's tone of voice was poisonously sweet.

"Not exactly," Dave said, on the defensive and resenting it. "We know what's on these twenty-five claims we call the Portland group, and the stuff is not very good. But once we tie them up with the forty-four, then we can interest a big outfit in developing them."

"Maybe I'm dumb," Abby said tartly, "but I always thought that a big outfit was interested in uranium. You got any? On this Portland group, you say it's not very good. And the forty-four you don't know." She paused and said scathingly, "Big deal."

Dave glanced at Dr. Channon. Stripped of hopes, hunches and dreams, his plans as stated by Abby did seem a bit adolescent, but there was no irony reflected in Dr. Channon's eyes.

"Why don't you get married before you go?" Dr. Channon asked.

It was Abby who found her voice first. "Marry a prospector? Never. If he was a short-order cook or a plumber's apprentice, I'd say yes in a second, but when he's crazy with uranium, not ever." She started out of the room, halted, turned, kissed him in a sisterly fashion and then announced, "I liked you selling asphalt tile, but if you're going to turn into the man with the hoe looking for uranium, you're on your own. Write me, Dave, if they sell such a thing as a postcard there." She went upstairs.

Dave and Dr. Channon exchanged a look of understanding and Dave leaned forward in his chair, elbows on his knees. "You think I'm crazy, Dr. Channon?"

Dr. Channon shrugged. "Sometimes I get a little tired myself of wearing a necktie. It's pretty late for me to change, though."

"It's not too late for me," Dave said almost grimly. "I hate to confess this nasty flaw in my character, but I don't like selling things. I guess I never did. When I have nightmares now, I'm running from people — customers. When I have a good dream, I'm always alone." He grinned at Dr. Channon. "Prescribe for that, doctor."

"You've probably got as good a prescription already as I could give you," Dr. Channon answered. Dr. Channon stood up now, and Dave knew Doc was on his side. Dr. Channon said, "I suppose this is the wrong time to ask you if there'll be a September wedding."

"Ask Abby."

"I sort of hoped she'd take to my suggestion," Dr. Channon said. He shook his head. "She'll be missing a lot of fun." He extended his hand now and added, "Good hunting, Dave."

They walked to the door together and Dave was about to say good night when Abby called from upstairs, "Wait a minute, Dave."

Doc smiled, turned and went back into the kitchen as Abby, in a white dressing gown, came down the stairs. She walked slowly up to Dave and said contritely, "I'm sorry I flipped my lid, Dave."

"You could always make up for that by marrying me."

Abby shook her head. "Any gal who marries a man without a job ought to have her head shrunk. If you think I can support you on what Dad pays me as a receptionist, you're crazy."

"Look, honey," Dave said quietly, "they buy uranium, remember? They pay money for it."

"You got any?"

"I will have."

Abby stood on tiptoe and kissed him, then said, "There, there. Why don't you go home and sleep on this? Sleep a year if you have to."

"Come on over to Joash next week-end," Dave coaxed.

"Unlikely," Abby said.

"All the same, I'll be in town Saturday."

Abby sighed. "You're sweet," she said softly. "I just wish you had some sense."

Abby was wrong when she said that somewhere on the way to Utah Dave would trade in his car for a jeep. He traded it in Ute City the next day for a new blue jeep and headed over the mountains for the desert beyond. Breaking the new motor in, he got barely into Utah by nightfall and spent the night in a motel. By early morning he had reached Joash, the small tree-shaded Mormon town that within a year had changed from a sheepherder's supply point into the capital of the uranium boom.

The paved highway which made a right-angle turn in the middle of town was thronged with cars, pickups and trucks, and Dave got stuck behind a lowboy carrying a dozer and compressor. He traveled three blocks at three miles an hour and finally dodged into a parking space.

Joash's business district was comprised of four blocks of business buildings and stores. Even the buildings seemed caught by the surprise of this boom, Dave thought, as he climbed out of the jeep into the hot sunshine. Old buildings with high plate glass windows and ornate cornices stood cheek by jowl with the new cinderblock-and-stucco affairs. The sidewalks were crowded, mostly with men, and the license plates of the parked cars were from twenty different states.

Dave shouldered his way into a food market and stocked up on food for himself, Bates Wallen, the geologist for Rex Uranium, and Hutch Elden, the taciturn and sun-dried old ranchhand who was his helper. Lugging the grub back to the jeep, Dave said hello to a girl in a waitress' uniform who worked at one of the eating joints. During the last month he had been in and out of Joash just enough to begin to place a few faces. He was loading the groceries in the jeep, his back to the street, when he heard a voice say, "Well, well, I see where Rex Uranium has just levied a new stock assessment."

Dave looked over his shoulder and saw a portly man dressed in well-pressed gabardines and dust-colored Stetson standing on the curb.

"Hello, Mr. Cushing," Dave said, and came over to shake hands. Dave had met Cushing through Wallen. The elderly man was a figure of note in Joash, an oil man who had switched to uranium and whose company, Cushing Minerals, was a fabulously shrewd operator in uranium exploration and development.

"Who said Rex had an assessment?" Dave asked.

"I just noticed the new jeep."

Cushing's full face was ruddy with good living, but looking down at him Dave noticed the affectionate amusement in his eyes.

"How you boys doing?" the old man asked.

"Well, we're afloat and still meeting the payroll," Dave said.

Cushing nodded sympathetically. "If you can do

21

that long enough, you're liable to hit."

"I think we have now," Dave said, and saw immediate interest in Cushing's eyes. "We're staking a group of forty-four claims this week."

Cushing was too old a timer to ask where, knowing that any answer he received would be a lie.

"Have you sampled?"

Dave nodded. "The assays should be out at camp now."

"If they're any good, give us a look at them," Cushing said, and then added, "Is it true you've leased Packard's Portland group?"

Dave nodded. "A couple of weeks ago. We took over from Reynolds what he had in it."

Cushing shook his head. "Personally I think it's a dog. I just don't like that country, but I wish you luck." He put out his hand. "Give my best to Wallen, and good luck, son."

As Dave headed south out of town, past the quiet side streets under the big cottonwoods, Cushing's words, "I don't like that country" still stuck in his mind. If, privately, Cushing thought the Portland group was a dog, so did Dave. It had been his first mistake after Rex Uranium was organized. In the flush of sudden wealth from the first assessment of the stockholders, Dave had decided to take over the lease of the Portland group from a man who had little interest in developing them. The samples which he had directed Wallen to take of the twenty-five claims comprising the Portland group had been only mediocre, but Dave had been unable to resist the bargain. The terms of the lease which he had taken over seemed good at the time. Rex Uranium had paid three thousand dollars for the lease which then had two months to run. At the end of that time, he could exercise his option to buy the group for one hundred thousand dollars, or renew the lease for another four months, providing Rex Uranium had done fifteen thousand dollars' worth of development work or paid its equivalent in cash or a combination of development work and cash.

Today there was barely a month of the lease left, and Dave knew its leasing had been a greenhorn's error. The expense of setting up Rex's operations and keeping Wallen and the men he needed exploring in the field had been more than Dave had anticipated; he had been unable to afford time, money, or work on the Portland group. Beyond that, the new claims overshadowed everything else. He could write off the Portland group as a bad investment and concentrate Rex Uranium's time and money on the big group.

From his boner on Portland, he had learned the lesson of frugality. Instead of spending time and money staking out the new group, he had left orders with Warren to sample first. If the assays were good, but only if they were good, Wallen was to start staking.

The driving claimed his full attention now. Forty miles south of Joash he had left the paved highway for a gravel road which had been pounded into a rocky corduroy by the heavy ore trucks from the surrounding canyons and mesas. As another hour passed, the road got rougher and small off-shoot roads, really only jeep trails, took off into the piñon and cedar. Some were marked by a tree blaze or a colored handkerchief, and now Dave began to look for Wallen's jeep trail. When he spotted it, he swung off west and for the next hour drove through a rolling country of thick cedar. Afterwards, the trail dived into a dry, boulder-strewn arroyo and from here on Dave crawled at a snail's pace. The road, if it could be called that, was worse than Dave remembered. It took all his skill now to keep from gutting the jeep on jagged rock shelves and boulders. Twice he high-centered, hanging the jeep on its frame so that the wheels could get no grip; in the blinding heat he was forced to build a rock bridge on which the jeep could lift itself free. Presently the offshoot canyon he was traveling joined the bigger canyon which had a more precipitous grade and which seemed to hold a still heat that was almost a hot liquid.

Bucking, sliding and crawling at a pace slower than a walk, his jeep ran out of this canyon into a larger one whose sheer walls lifted a hundred feet high on either bank of its sandy bed. Still keeping west, Dave traveled the canyon, clinging to the shady side when he could. Even with the sun heeled over into late afternoon, the rocks held the heat and Dave found himself panting like a dog.

A subtle change began to come over the country and the canyon widened; rock gave way to gravel which held stunted piñon and great clusters of prickly pear. Now the jeep tracks which he had been following cut up the precipitous left bank. Dave had to make two runs before his grinding jeep achieved the rim. A mile beyond and to the south in a stand of tall cedars lay the camp and the tent, and in the lowering dusk Dave smelled the smoke of the campfire even before he saw it.

Wallen and Hutch had heard the jeep a half-hour before Dave pulled into sight between the ragged cedars; they were standing by the fire waiting, their own battered jeep in the background.

Dave cut the motor, groaned and stepped out while Wallen, a big man in sweat-stained suntans, came over.

"Welcome, president," he murmured mockingly as he held out his hand to Dave. He was, Dave knew, eyeing the new jeep with covetous eyes. Dave had already guessed Wallen's age at thirty. He was a big-boned man of over six feet with an almost round head, topped by pale hair closely cropped. His head appeared to grow out of his high shoulders since he had almost no neck, and he was sunburned such a deep red that his amiable face seemed stained.

"Couldn't you guys find a harder place to get to?" Dave said, and Wallen laughed.

Behind Wallen, Hutch Elden, with a back-country shyness, waited until Dave looked at him and extended his hand.

"Hutch, you're getting fat," Dave said.

This brought a faint smile to Hutch's creased

and sun-blackened face. He was a lath of a man with hands the size of a fielder's glove; his waist overalls were gray with age and his sun-faded blue shirt was white rimmed with the salt of his sweat. Under his battered Stetson, the color of the dust around him, were the palest eyes Dave had ever seen and they were deep-set under bushy gray brows. His homely face was covered clear to the cheekbones with a white beard stubble.

"You never should of brought anything that new out here," Hutch said, tilting his head toward the jeep. "Hell, these dude prospectors will shoot you for a second-hand one."

Dave grinned. "Next trip we'll have it gold-plated."

He saw Wallen and Hutch exchange glances, but thought nothing of it. The three of them stepped over to the jeep and unloaded Dave's grub and bedroll. From his box of food he pulled out a sack of grapes which brought a momentary pleasure to Hutch's eyes. Hutch stirred up the fire, put the blackened coffeepot on it while Dave assembled a sandwich from the food he had brought. Once the first edge of his hunger was gone, he asked, "Well, how did the staking go?"

Wallen was seated across the fire in the lowering dusk and now Dave regarded him, waiting for the account of their labors.

"It didn't go," Wallen said quietly.

Dave scowled. "What does that mean?"

"We didn't stake it."

Dave felt surprise, dismay and then anger as

he watched Wallen. "Why in the hell not?" he demanded.

For answer Wallen rose and went into the weathered tent stretched on a rope between two piñons. Dave glanced at Hutch sprawled out on the ground, leaning on an elbow. The expression on Hutch's face was unreadable. Wallen returned now with a sheaf of papers. Then extending them to Dave, he said, "Here's the assayer's report on the seventy-six samples we took."

Dave had a premonition of what was coming. His glance fell to the top assay and he noted that the percentage of uranium oxide contained in that sample was .053. Leafing through the sheets, quickly at first and then more slowly, he saw that some samples held a thousandth percentage more and many held less. These percentages of uranium, Dave knew bitterly, were not worth mining. In other words, the group upon which Rex Uranium would build its fortunes was worthless, just so much real estate without value.

For a moment Dave felt an actual physical sickness. He and Wallen had felt so sure, so very sure, that the ore-bearing rock Wallen had found on the Portland group would be richer in the new group which lay to the south of the Portland group. Too stunned to speak now, he stared down at the reports and memory goaded him. *"Remember, they buy uranium?"* he had reminded Abby the other night, and Abby had asked, *"You got any?"*

Hutch's voice interrupted his bitter thoughts. "We took seventy-six samples, all told," Hutch said. "We covered that damn country like a heavy rain. It stands all on end and you couldn't even get a burro into it." He paused. "Bates did the sampling while I carried the samples out on my back and, by Harry, I'm still rump-sprung."

Still Dave was silent, trying to accept this. The new group was to be the big find, justifying his muff of the Portland lease, the shrugging off of the loss of his job and the bitter quarrel with Abby. Now Dave knew they were where they started weeks ago, a little wiser but lacking any luck at all.

He regarded Wallen now. "You think you really covered it, Bates?"

"The best I know how, and I *know* how," Bates replied.

"What do you think we should do with them?"

"Forget them."

"But if there's that percentage of stuff on the surface, it's bound to get better underneath," Dave said stubbornly.

Bates grinned but without humor. "There's one way to find out."

"Yeah, I know, diamond drilling."

Bates nodded in agreement and they were both silent. Diamond drilling, the shortest cut to proof of ore, was a financial luxury they both knew Rex Uranium could not afford. By drilling down through the overburden of soil, sand and rock, the hollow drill would come up with the core of everything it had passed through. By testing this core it could be determined at what depth the ore was lying and what grade the ore was. The only other way to find out, Dave knew, was by the laborious, time-consuming and expensively risky method of sinking a shaft and sampling what was found. There was, Dave knew, no guarantee at all that the percentage would be better in the ore under the surface unless they could prove it by expensive diamond drilling.

He saw in the geologist's face the same defeat that must have been in his own. Then on impulse he said, "Let's stake them anyway, Bates."

"And do what with it?"

"All right, we'll call in the Atomic Energy Commission boys to look it over. Or call in the big companies."

"Before either one of them would consider it, they'll want to look at your assays. That," he said dryly, "is when they laugh in your face."

Dave knew this was true, but he said, even more stubbornly, "Let's stake it."

A momentary irritation flicked in Wallen's eyes. "You're president of this outfit, Dave, and I'm under your orders. If you order me to stake, you've got my resignation right now."

Dave was surprised at the quiet vehemence in his tone. He glanced at Hutch, whose sleepy, pale eyes were unreadable.

"You feel that strongly about it?"

"I do."

"Why?"

"In the first place I'm a trained geologist and you're not. You're questioning my professional ability."

"I didn't mean to," Dave said quietly. "I really mean that, Bates."

"I know you didn't." Bates was silent a moment. "Trouble was, Dave, we were fooled by mass reaction."

"What's that?"

"Our Geiger indicated pretty good ore. Actually it was picking up a lot of radioactivity from a mass of low-grade stuff, and that tricks you into thinking you're really on to something good. The only way to really find out the truth is to sample, and we did. It just isn't worth staking." He paused. "I've got a 5 percent interest in Rex myself. If I thought this group would make me money, wouldn't I stake it?"

His glance held Dave's and finally Dave looked away. Everything Wallen said was true, Dave knew. Rex Uranium was buying Wallen's professional knowledge and only a green and untrained fool like himself would dream of going against his word. Dave tried in that moment to analyze his feeling about staking these claims. Was it a hunch that they contained good ore, or was it plain stubbornness brought on by this disappointing news? He couldn't tell, but he did know that he had pushed Wallen into almost open anger. He also knew that he was stubbornly refusing to recognize disaster.

It was full dark now and Dave watched Wallen across the campfire. Then he asked the question which had to come sooner or later. "What do you want to do now, Bates?"

"I'd like to move south and across the river."

The river, of course, was the Colorado, and Dave knew that such a move would mean writing off the weeks of work here and starting all over again.

"What about mining the Portland group?"

"You want a straight answer, Dave?"

Dave nodded wearily.

"Our assays on Portland were lousy. You've got less than a month before your lease is up. You think in that time you could mine fifteen thousand dollars worth of ore or raise the cash to renew the lease?"

"I don't know. I can tell you don't think so, though."

"That's right."

There was, Dave thought, nothing left to do but eat and go to bed.

"Tell you what," Dave said to Wallen after breakfast next morning, "why don't you take the new jeep in this morning and let Hutch and me break camp? The way I feel now, it might even take us a couple of days."

"Sounds good," Wallen said. They were stalling over their second cup of coffee in the still cool morning. "If you're not in a hurry, Dave, I'd like to take in a couple of sessions of this Uranium Miners Association meeting this week-end."

"What's that?"

"It was formed a couple of months ago by the small outfits who think they're getting clipped on the ore sampling methods of the milling companies. I'm curious to see what they're going to do about it."

"Then clear out," Dave said. "We'll see you in Joash."

A half-hour later Wallen pulled out of camp, and the sound of his motor had not yet died before Dave was tramping over to the company jeep. From its padded box, he lifted out the Geiger Counter, then returned to the fire.

Hutch was watching him carefully as Dave halted before him and said, "Guess."

Hutch's seamed face held no expression at all. "You think Wallen's wrong."

"All I know is what I saw on the Geiger when we were first in there," Dave said thinly. "If you want to come along, Hutch, grab some sample sacks."

"Suits me," Hutch answered tranquilly.

Hutch filled the canteen with water, threw a couple of cans of tomatoes, the old cowpuncher's favorite fruit, into his pack sack and was ready to go. Dave slung the Geiger Counter over his shoulder, took the battered prospector's pick and joined him, and they headed southeast out of camp. Within ten minutes' walk they were climbing in and out of sheer-sided canyons whose floors were strewn with boulders half as big as a small house. Hutch traveled his easy, tireless but mile-eating pace. As the going got rougher, Dave marveled that any human could pack out the weight in samples that Hutch had moved. They rested ten minutes out of the hour, which was just long enough for a cigarette and for Dave's rubbery legs to cease trembling.

On ahead of them was a long hogback running perhaps two miles on the north-south axis, sparsely covered with piñon and of reddish brown sandstone. Dave recognized this ridge as their goal, yet they were a good hour from it. At its north and over the ridge lay the Portland group. The new group, as Wallen had planned the staking last week, lay to the south and straddled the ridge.

As he labored behind Hutch, Dave wondered if he was on a foolish errand. The greenest prospector fresh out of Brooklyn could turn up rock that kicked the Geiger Counter. It was another matter, however, to interpret the geology which alone could make sense of the Geiger readings. Still, in his own bungling fashion he was going to satisfy himself, he thought.

Slowly they approached, through the rough, climbing country, just to the base of the ridge. Suddenly Hutch halted so abruptly that Dave bumped into him. Hutch was looking at something off to his right among the piñons, and when Dave looked, he saw nothing. Wordlessly then Hutch cut over into the scattered piñons and then Dave saw the new pale-wood chips at the base of a tree that had attracted Hutch's attention. The lower branches of the tree had been trimmed and as they approached they saw a blaze on a trunk and the white of a card.

They approached together and Dave saw that

this was a form location notice. Briefly it said that this was the northeast corner of Claim 24, called Gentle George and recorded by Tri-State Uranium, Box 370, Joash, Utah.

Dave glanced at Hutch, puzzled. "Was that here when you left?"

Hutch shook his head in negation and for a puzzled moment the two men looked at each other.

Dave said, "Something's betting Bates is wrong."

Hutch said nothing. They turned south and began to walk, and in a few minutes they came to the peeled four-foot-high stake which proclaimed a common corner for Claim 24 and 23.

Dave looked bleakly at the location notice, then at the ridge looming ahead, and then at Hutch.

"Who's Tri-State?" he asked.

"A big outfit," Hutch said. "One of the biggest."

Where Wallen had found nothing worth staking, a big outfit had, Dave thought bitterly, and he said to Hutch, "If they stake, they must think there's something here."

"That don't put it here," Hutch said.

It was true, Dave thought, and he looked again at the ridge. Then he said thinly, "If it takes me a year, Hutch, I'm going to find out what they thought was worth staking. Come along."

He turned uphill toward the ridge, picking his way through scattered piñon and following the course of a dry stream bed that would lead him up the canyon. Presently, as the walls began to rise, he unslung his Geiger Counter, switched it on and slowly began to travel up the canyon, holding the Geiger probe against the rock. He was so intent on watching the dial, Hutch had to speak. "Hold it, Dave," Hutch said very quietly.

Dave turned, puzzled, and he saw Hutch looking beyond him. Now Dave swiveled his head.

Up canyon were three men. Two of them wore soiled suntans and straw Stetsons, and the youngest of these two held a carbine slacked at his side. But the third man was the man Dave's attention settled upon. He was tall and wide, with a deep chest that merged into an ample belly, and his tailored suntans were almost foppish in cut. His straw Stetson was white and fresh as paint over a heavy, full-jawed and swarthy face.

At Dave's hello none of them spoke; the heavy man tramped toward him, and the others followed. Dave felt a faint stirring of apprehension and waited until the heavy man hauled up before him. The man's eyes were what Dave watched now; they were pale and bleak, the eyes of a storm trooper or the eyes of a corrupt cop who had seen everything and believed nothing.

"Finding all the uranium you want, Jack?" he asked in a deceptively pleasant voice.

"Just looking around," Dave answered.

"This ground's staked."

"I know. Our claims adjoin yours to the north over the ridge. I'm trying to get a lead on where to hunt for our stuff."

"Well, well, you got some land to prospect on, have you?"

Dave didn't answer, and the heavy man turned to the one carrying the rifle, "Put the gun on him, Fred." He only looked briefly, understandingly at the third man, who stepped away.

"You look like an old-time prospector, Jack," the heavy man went on pleasantly. "Tell me about your adventures in the West."

Hutch said quietly from behind Dave, "Let's go, Dave."

"You aren't going anywhere, Pappy," the heavy man said to Hutch.

"Look," Dave began, "we haven't touched your monuments or claim notices. We're trespassing. If you want us off, we'll get off."

"He says he'll get off, Chief," the third man said softly.

"I heard him," Chief said. Suddenly the third man jumped on Dave's back, pinning his arms, and Dave saw Fred's carbine come up, pointed at Hutch. Now the heavy man gave Dave a back-handed cuff across the face.

"Like that, Jack?" Chief asked.

A blind anger rose in Dave, and he struggled to break the man's grip. Then Chief, laughing, slapped his face time and time again with the palm of his hand and the back of his hand. Then, suddenly, he drove his massive fist into Dave's solar plexus.

The third man released his hold and now Dave fell to his knees, fighting agonizingly for breath. Deaf to everything around him, he gagged for what seemed an eternity in an effort to get air into his lungs. He sensed, but hardly felt, the boot against his side as Chief roughly turned him over on his side. Presently sanity began to return slowly as Dave once more began to breathe. He heard Chief say, "Get up, Jack, before I kick your head off."

Slowly Dave struggled to his knees and he felt Hutch's arm around him, hoisting him to his feet.

"This is just a mussing up, Jack," Chief said cheerfully. "Next time we'll work you over. Now get out of here."

It was Hutch who turned him and guided him, stumbling, back down the canyon.

2

There were all manner and sizes of trailers spotted around the dusty, empty lots of Joash; they came and went as birds of passage with their prospector and geologist owners moving in and out from the field. Their owners had no real life in the town; their few acquaintances consisted of waitresses, courthouse workers, gas station attendants and the night operators at the telephone exchange which was jammed till past midnight each evening. They were an impersonal lot, secretive and tireless, busy during the day and retreating to their trailers in the early evening.

One group of four trailers located on an empty corner lot on a quiet side street and seemed to evidence more permanency than the others. They ranged in an orderly line across the back of the lot and the earth was still raw where water connections had been brought in from the street. The fore part of the lot held two power wagons and two jeeps all painted with the name Tri-State Exploration, Inc., across the engine hoods. The trailers were unmarked, although all of the vehicles bore Utah license plates. The largest trailer, aluminum and almost as big as a box car, had a tall radio mast beside it and telephone wires slanting down to it.

It was close to 6 o'clock of the hot afternoon when a black Cadillac convertible, a diminutive Filipino man at the wheel, swung off the quiet street into the lot and halted. The other passenger was a woman and she sat motionless a moment, regarding the bleak lot, the dirt-crusted vehicles, and finally the trailers. When the Filipino had circled the car and opened the door, she stepped out and there was still an expressionless appraisal in her dark eyes. She might have been twenty-five and her hair, worn pony-tail fashion, was so pale it had almost no color. Her eyebrows and long eyelashes were black, her nose perhaps a little too short, but otherwise she was beautiful in the characterless over-groomed manner of a fashion magazine model.

Now the door to the big trailer opened, and a man in clean suntans stepped out and headed for the car. He was short, grizzled, middle-aged and deeply tanned, and he extended his hand as he approached, saying, "Hello, Mrs. Heath. It's nice to see you."

Mrs. Heath held out her hand and said, "How've you been, Scott?" The lack of real cordiality in her greeting put a certain reserve in the man's face. He gestured toward the trailer and fell in beside her, afterward opening the trailer door.

The interior of the huge vehicle was a combination lounge and office. Its pale leather walls were lined with maps and beyond the semicircular lounge were two desks, a drafting board and in the rear bay a complicated mass of radio equipment. There were telephones on the desk, fluorescent lights overhead and the reassuring hum of the air conditioner.

A pretty young secretary was working at the nearest desk and now she looked up and smiled. "Welcome home, Mrs. Heath."

The woman smiled faintly. "That's a nice sentiment, Joyce, but I'm glad it isn't home."

The secretary smiled uncertainly and went on with her typing. Mrs. Heath sank down on the lounge.

Scott Everson was Tri-State's head geologist; left to choose his own office, he would have demanded only a corner of a room at the Tri-State Uranium mine fifty miles to the south. However, Mrs. Heath had insisted long ago that the exploration and mining divisions should be housed separately, and these trailers were doing service as the exploration office until the big cinderblock Tri-State building was completed on the edge of Joash. He could have done without all the plush, too, but he went through the well-rehearsed duties entailed by any visit of Mrs. Heath. At the small bar in the corner he poured a Scotch on the rocks for Mrs. Heath, delivered it, lighted her cigarette and then inquired, "Nice trip?"

"Foul," Mrs. Heath said briefly, dismissing the subject. She studied Scott Everson with brief appraisal as if waiting for him to begin speaking about a subject they both knew he was going to talk about. Everson, however, crossed her up. "You know you don't really have to take that beating, Mrs. Heath. This air strip is good and it's no time at all to the Coast."

"I suppose you're right," Mrs. Heath said indifferently, and sipped her drink. Then she said, "Anything new since I called last night?"

Everson smiled faintly. "New, but expected. Borthen came over on the Red Ledge property today."

Mrs. Heath's dark eyebrows lifted. "Trouble?"

"Chief booted him off."

"Did he have to get rough?"

"I guess there was a scuffle. Nothing serious."

Mrs. Heath smiled faintly at that. "How does it look?"

"From thirty samples we've had run, I think it's pretty special," Everson replied. "We kept the assayer up for two nights so we're having to give him some sleep before the rest of the assays can be run."

"Has Wallen been in?"

"I saw him on the street today, so he ought to be in tonight."

"Did he speak to you?"

"No recognition at all."

"That's good," Mrs. Heath said quietly. "Maybe I underestimated him. He impressed me as being just thick enough to shake hands with you right in front of Borthen."

She finished her drink now and rose. Everson rose, too. Now Mrs. Heath said, "Will you join me for dinner, Scott?"

"Happy to," Everson replied quietly.

Without further comment, she headed for the door, preceded by Everson.

In a moment he returned and Joyce ceased her typing. They regarded each other for a silent moment and on Joyce's pretty face was an expression of sardonic distaste.

Everson said dryly, "You ought to hide your emotions a little more skillfully, Joyce."

"I know I should, but I can't," Joyce said grimly. "Every time I see her I keep looking for those five stars she ought to be wearing on her shoulders."

Joyce drew out a cigarette, lighted it, then put an arm over the back of her chair. "I've only been working here two months. Do you think she knows my name?"

"She knows everything about you."

Joyce looked at him skeptically. "Not half as much as I know about her."

Everson looked at her disapprovingly. "Just what do you know about her?"

"I don't mean I know anything special, but just what I've read in all the columns. She was in a chorus line and sang in a night club before her husband traded her in."

"That's honest work."

"Sure, but why doesn't she stay there? What's she doing in a man's racket, anyway?"

Everson smiled and said dryly, "She's doing very well I'd say. The trouble with you, Joyce, you don't know anything about her. For instance, do you know what she was doing in her spare time when she was in a chorus line?"

"Please, Mr. Everson, let's keep this conversation on a high level," Joyce said mockingly.

"You're flip, but I'm serious. During her off hours she ran two dress shops that she picked up for a song and that put her on her feet in a big way."

Joyce looked surprised. "Who says?"

"She told me."

Joyce smoked a moment in silence. "Could be," she conceded. "She didn't pick up all this business know-how at the Stork Club." Joyce thought a moment longer. "No wonder her guy flaked her off. Who wants to be married to a comptometer?"

"It was the other way round," Everson said firmly. "He chased around until she couldn't put up with it any longer."

"Sure," Joyce said skeptically. "I'll bet she had a broken heart that took about three million in alimony to cure."

"You're wrong again," Everson said with asperity. "She sat down with Heath's lawyers and looked at his whole portfolio of holdings. Instead of belting him for a six-figure alimony she chose shares in a business that she wanted to run herself, which was Tri-State." He paused. "Does that tell you anything, my girl?"

"Should it?"

"It tells me plenty," Everson said now, his voice sharp. "It tells me she's no ordinary good-looking tramp interested only in clothes. She was a business woman before her marriage and a business woman afterwards."

43

"And only a business woman," Joyce said. "As far as that goes you can leave off the woman. She's business."

"She pays your salary, doesn't she?" Everson said, almost angrily.

"She pays me twice as much as other girls get for doing three girls' work," Joyce said tartly. "Come to think of it, when do I get some help, Mr. Everson? Have you looked at your watch?"

"I know, I know," Everson said placatingly. "The hours are bad, but give us time to get another good girl, will you?"

Joyce stubbed out her cigarette. "Flattery has won me again," she said dryly, and went back to her typing.

It was an hour later and full dark when Everson and Holly Heath were served coffee and brandy by Perez, the Filipino house boy, in Mrs. Heath's own trailer. Everson marveled that such a meal could be produced in the tiny kitchen and on a stove the size of a silver dollar, but the evidence was undeniable.

Mrs. Heath wore a fresh-looking off-the-shoulder, blue linen dress that Everson guessed cost the equivalent of his last month's salary. On the other hand, he corrected himself, with her knowledge of clothes it could have been picked up by a smart shopper for eight and a half bucks. Whatever it cost, she looked beautiful in it and was altogether pleasant on the eyes. *But upon the ears, no,* Everson thought.

Everson waited until Perez offered him a cigar

and left the trailer before he settled down to his real news.

"I've saved the most important news for you until we could be alone, Mrs. Heath."

Holly Heath waited.

"You remember we flew a scintillometer survey over that Red Ledge group after Wallen tipped us off?"

Mrs. Heath nodded.

"I noticed then that as we made our approach on the group, we were picking up some reaction from the Portland group that Borthen is leasing. Last week I went in by myself on a hunch." He paused, smiling a little. "I don't think that group has been geologized since Packard leased it."

"Didn't Borthen?"

"He couldn't have," Everson said dryly. "A hundred feet of rimrock has caved off recently. It's exposed about a fifty foot long outcrop of high-grade ore in the channel and it runs up to sixteen feet thick." Everson could not keep the excitement out of his voice. "Nothing on the Red Ledge will touch it for grade, and I think tonnage."

Mrs. Heath was silent a long moment. "Who knows this?"

"Not a soul."

"Not Wallen? He must have made a reconnaissance."

"My guess is that Wallen dogged it, as usual. Rex is a poor boy's oufit and I know they couldn't afford to fly it with the scintillometer. Wallen

45

probably grab-sampled the stuff on the flats and let it go at that."

"How long has Borthen's lease to run?"

"Around a month. He's got development work to do or cash to raise if he's to renew his lease."

Holly Heath smiled. "You think he can?"

"I'm sure he can't."

"Then we simply wait him out and buy from Packard, is that it?"

Everson nodded. Mrs. Heath was silent for some time, savoring this. The irony of it appealed to her. Borthen, who had been maneuvered out of the Red Ledge group, was sitting on a fortune that he didn't know existed and would probably let go by default.

Everson said then, "May I ask a favor, Mrs. Heath?"

"Of course."

"I don't like to complain, but this rough stuff of Chief's is something I don't like. I know you value him as your bodyguard, but to be frank with you, he had no business being up there. We could have handled Borthen without any trouble."

"I disagree," Holly Heath said coldly. "Certain situations call for a show of force. If you're big, act big."

Everson shrugged. "Suit yourself."

"I intend to."

There was a knock on the door and Perez stuck his head in and said, "Man to see you, Mrs. Heath."

She rose, as did Everson, who asked, "Want me along?"

"I think not. It will be less embarrassing this way."

"Then thank you for dinner," Everson said politely.

Holly Heath nodded and went out. She skirted the trailer, stumbling in her high-heel shoes on the uneven ground. Her head was still full of Everson's news, and she felt the old excitement stirring within her.

When she had received Everson's call relaying Wallen's news of the Red Ledge discovery she had hurried out here. This was the sort of situation she loved, a cutthroat, fast-moving foray with a lot of money at stake, but now Everson's news of the Portland group made it even more exciting. Now she could tangle the skein until her motives were obscured, using her looks and her money to get what she wanted. The workaday business of directing a mine was fun in a way, but the quick raid, the use of intrigue and guile, the ruthless kill, was more fun. But the most fun of all was in knowing that men, in their vanity, thought of her only as beautiful and desirable, until it was too late for them to realize that a sharper brain than theirs lay behind the beauty.

Stepping into the office trailer, she greeted Wallen pleasantly. He was dressed in clean suntans and he rose lazily at her entrance.

"Please sit down, Mr. Wallen." She sank onto the lounge and watched him slack his big hulk into the seat opposite her. He had a certain animal magnetism about him, Holly decided, and the curious charm of an admitted scoundrel, but he was unbelievably stupid. "You seem to have carried this off nicely. Did Borthen suspect anything?" she asked.

Wallen grinned easily. "He wanted to stake in spite of the assays. I waved the flag of professional honor and he backed down."

"Not all the way," Holly Heath observed. "We threw him off the property today." She paused. "Where does that leave you?"

Wallen scowled. "I'll tell him anybody can stake ground, but it doesn't necessarily mean there's uranium there. I'll still have the assays to back me up."

"What did you sample, dirt?"

"Country rock mostly, with a very low count."

They smiled at each other in mutual satisfaction. Mrs. Heath opened her purse now and took out a salmon-colored slip of paper which she extended to Wallen. He looked at it, and saw it was a cashier's check for a thousand dollars. He slipped the check in his shirt pocket as Holly Heath rose and went over to her secretary's desk. She was aware Wallen was watching her, as, standing at the desk, she checked Joyce's copy of the agreement with Wallen which gave him in return for his treachery to Rex Uranium, 5 percent of the net of the value of all ores taken from the Red Ledge group.

Returning to the table, she extended the agreement to Wallen who slouched down in his seat and began to read while he absent-mindedly lighted a cigarette. Holly Heath watched him, remembering how she had acquired him. A year ago Everson and Wallen had attended a refresher session together at the School of Mines. Unexpectedly meeting one night, a month or so ago, Wallen had told Everson of his new job with Rex Uranium, a collection of innocents who were both ignorant and gullible. In contemptuously passing the story on to Holly Heath, Scott remarked that Wallen was dogging on his job and that he seemed to prefer to make a dollar the dishonest way. That had been enough for Holly Heath. Practical-minded, she saw where she could buy another firm's geologist for a moderate bribe without having to support him in the field.

Wallen flipped over the last page and tossed the agreement on the table. "It looks bulletproof," he observed. "We can make beautiful uranium together." He glanced over to the bar and added, "I think we ought to have a drink to seal it."

"Not for me, but help yourself," Holly Heath said coolly. She sat down now, as Wallen rose, moved over to the bar and mixed himself a drink. He lifted his glass to her and she acknowledged it with a faint smile. "What are Rex's plans now?" she asked almost indifferently.

"The tile salesman will go wherever I tell him to," Wallen said.

Holly Heath's question now seemed one of only idle curiosity. "Doesn't Rex have some sort of lease near us?"

"The Portland group," Wallen said scoffingly.

"He got suckered into leasing it and now it's too late to finish the development work. It's strictly Class B goat pasture anyway."

Holly Heath smiled at this. Apparently there was no cause for alarm, and she knew further questioning might arouse Wallen's curiosity.

She knew that Wallen, with the bland gall of the born moocher, would try to make himself at home here and she had no intention of encouraging him. She lit a cigarette and smoked in silence as Wallen, beginning to understand that he was not particularly welcome now that his business was finished, swiftly drank his highball.

"Thank you, Mrs. Heath. Any orders?"

"Just let me know where you decide to take your tile salesman."

Wallen grinned, flipped her a casual good-bye and went out.

Holly Heath picked up his glass and went over to the sink to rinse it, just as the door opened. Heaving his massive bulk up the step, Chief entered the trailer and, at sight of his employer, took off his hat.

Holly smiled briefly at him. She had not seen him since the night of Everson's call after which she had promptly had him flown to Joash to lend a hand in case of trouble at the staking of the Red Ledge group. "Have a nice vacation?"

"Fine, Mrs. Heath," Chief said, and then added, "Kind of different."

Holly looked at him levelly. "So I hear. What happened out there?"

"Just what you figured," Chief said, admiration in his voice. "I picked up a couple of the drillers and we waited on the ridge with binoculars. It was around noon when we saw them and we went down to meet them."

"And?"

Chief shrugged. "I told him it was private property, gave him a couple of cuffs and kicked him off."

Mrs. Heath nodded in approval. She wanted it made abundantly clear to Wallen's tile salesman that he was through with what was now Tri-State property. She wondered idly, as she dried the glass, what this Borthen was like. Since Wallen spoke of him so contemptuously and Chief had slapped him around, she pictured him as a sober and undersized man, probably the institutional-type salesman with delusions of grandeur.

She put the glass away and emptied the ashtray, then asked belatedly, "You got your room all right, Chief?"

"Just fine, Mrs. Heath."

"Then I'll see you in the morning," Holly Heath said. She gave him a smile, much as she would give a dog a good-night pat. She said good night and went out.

By bare dawn Dave and Hutch had broken camp. Their jeep piled high with gear, they were soon in the canyon maze that at this hour of the morning was blessedly cool.

Dave was glad to leave this hard-luck camp.

51

Everything that had happened to him there was bad, he thought grimly. It was there he had learned that Wallen had not staked and it was there he learned that somebody else had. It was to this camp he returned after being slugged and thrown off by the Tri-State crew. And in this camp last night he had come to the reluctant decision that Rex Uranium, because it had no other choice, must mine the Portland group.

Through the middle of the cloudless morning they nursed the ageing company jeep along the boulder-strewn canyon beds and took turns pushing it up the steeper grades. Dave was still rubber-legged from the nausea that had followed his beating at the hands of the Tri-State crew, and, what with the increasing heat of the morning, the shoddy jeep, and the lingering taste of defeat, his mood was foul and his temper edging him.

It was early afternoon when they pulled into Joash, which was hot and jammed not only with the usual Saturday crowd but with cars and trucks of the miners and prospectors who were attending the uranium meeting. Dave knew it was hopeless to try to get a room, and Hutch suggested the home of a friend of his on one of the quiet side streets.

When they arrived the house was locked, the friend absent, so Hutch appropriated the shed in the rear where they deposited their bedrolls among bits of old harness, a lawn mower, peach baskets and garden tools.

There were half a hundred things Dave knew

he must do, and he knew the one he wanted to do first. As soon as the jeep was unloaded, he bid Hutch good-bye and headed for the courthouse where the uranium miners were meeting. Mormon stone masons had fashioned this handsome old three-story building surrounded by huge cottonwood trees and set in a tiny close-clipped lawn. With difficulty, Dave found a parking spot, and wearily climbed out of the jeep. He was tired, unshaven, hungry, but above all, a kind of sodden anger was pushing him.

As he tramped up the walk he saw the backs of the men in the open windows of the second-floor courtroom where the meeting was taking place. On the second floor there was a crowd of men jamming the doorway and Dave stubbornly shouldered his way through them until he could see into the room. There was barely standing room left; every seat was taken and men filled the jury box. They had even shifted the attorney's tables against the wall to sit on.

Dave paid no attention to the droning voice of the chairman, but searched the room for Wallen. He was standing in the rear and, spotting him, Dave began to bull his way toward him. Halfway to the rear windows, Wallen saw him, and Dave beckoned him to come out. Dave retreated to the hall and walked down it out of earshot of the crowd, and, hands on hips, waited for Wallen.

Presently Wallen broke through the mob and came down the hall, an expression of concern on his face. Approaching Dave, he said, "What's up?"

"The group we passed up is staked," Dave said thinly.

"You and Hutch staked them?" Wallen asked.

"When we got there, they were staked by Tri-State Uranium."

Wallen's jaw set a little. "So what? Anybody can stake goat pasture."

"Anybody but us," Dave said grimly. "We have to pass it up."

Anger came into Wallen's face and when he spoke it was in his voice too. He made a sharp, choppy gesture with his hand, saying, "Look, Dave, you saw the assays. Show them to any mining man who knows and ask him if he'd stake. I won't argue about this anymore."

A kind of recklessness was pushing Dave now. "All right, we won't argue, but I'll make you a promise." He paused. "If Tri-State starts to develop that property, you'll be looking for a job."

"Fair enough," Bates said curtly.

"That's only one reason I hauled you out of the meeting," Dave said. "The other is, we're going to work."

"Where we going?"

"We're going to mine the Portland group."

A look of mixed alarm and disgust came into Wallen's face. Then he said, "Why?"

"It's pretty damn simple," Dave said meagerly. "We lost our crack at the big group. The Portland's all we got, unless we want to quit."

"There's other stuff."

"Sure," Dave said bitterly. "Stuff for other people to stake." He saw the anger flare in Wallen's eyes, but before Wallen could speak Dave went on. "I want you to start rounding up the stuff we'll need to start mining by Monday. You know more about this than I do, but we'll need a pneumatic jack hammer, drill steel, powder, fuse and caps, lumber, a wall tent and grub. Hutch is rounding up a couple of miners, a cook and a stove. We can rent a compressor, can't we?"

Wallen nodded sullenly.

"This is Saturday and everything will be closed up tomorrow. Now get going," Dave said.

Wallen shrugged. "You're the boss."

"You're damn right I am. Forget it, and you're in trouble." He waited a moment to see if Wallen would answer and when he did not, Dave walked past him and downstairs. For the hundredth time, he wished passionately that he knew if Wallen was right in refusing to stake. And, remembering the smug way in which Wallen hid behind the assays, he almost hated him.

Once outside, he forgot him and put his mind to the second order of business. At a downtown filling station he inquired for the office of Tri-State Uranium and was asked if he meant the mine or the exploration office. Remembering that the crew who had booted him off were probably the staking crew, he said the exploration office, and was directed to the lot housing the trailers.

Pulling into the lot, Dave looked at the setup with momentary puzzlement, then got out and headed for the biggest trailer under the radio mast. At his knock a voice called, "Come in," and Dave stepped into the trailer. For a brief moment Dave was almost awed by the size and luxury of the interior; absurdly enough, there was even a thick-piled beige-colored carpet under foot. A slight, middle-aged man, wearing horn-rimmed glasses was standing beyond the leather lounge, dictating to a blonde secretary. He looked at Dave inquiringly.

Dave tramped toward him, saying, "My name's Borthen and I want to see the man who directs your staking."

"Staking where?"

When Dave told him, the man's face altered faintly into grimness. "Mrs. Heath is in charge of all Tri-State operations."

Dave scowled. "Mrs. Heath?" he asked, surprise in his voice, and he looked at the secretary.

"She's not here," the man said.

"All right, I'll wait for her," Dave said grimly.

"Is there anything I can do for you?"

"Not anything."

The man exchanged glances with his secretary and a look of exasperation came into his face, "Mrs. Heath won't be back until 6 o'clock."

"I'll wait for her," Dave said stubbornly.

The man sighed. "Look," he began patiently, "Mrs. Heath is at the mine. She won't be home until after we're closed up."

"I'll wait for her," Dave repeated.

The man looked at him a long moment, and

then said, "Will your business take long?"

"No."

"I'm driving out in a few minutes. Come along if you want, but I've got to be back here by four. Otherwise, if your business can't wait, I'd suggest you drive out yourself."

Remembering the slowness of the ancient jeep, Dave said, "I'll ride with you."

"Then I'll be with you as soon as I'm finished."

Dave stepped out and moved over into the shade of the tall cottonwoods, and presently the man came out and headed for a new sedan. Dave followed him. When they were seated the man extended his hand, saying, "We might as well get acquainted. My name's Everson. I'm geologist for Tri-State."

"Dave Borthen."

They shook hands and Everson drove off. For forty miles they kept on the paved highway which ran around high flat-topped mesas and occasionally bridged deep-red sandstone canyons.

Dave wondered what he had let himself in for, in deciding to see this woman. She was probably an eccentric old harridan who had little control over the men working for her, but he was grimly determined not to be put off.

Three-quarters of an hour later they turned off the main highway into a wide-mouth canyon whose red sandstone sides held stunted piñon and cedar. Big, heavily loaded ore trucks passed them, raising clouds of red dust. As they climbed the canyon through the haze of dust, Dave presently saw the towering timber head frame which loomed

57

over Tri-State's original discovery shaft and which carried the cable sheaves for hoisting ore. As they drove closer, Dave saw that the vertical shaft had been abandoned for a wide-mouthed horizontal tunnel driven in from downslope below the original discovery cut. Huge diesel shuttle cars drove out of the tunnel dumping their load of rock on a massive stock pile, circled and went back into the tunnel. A dozer was unceasingly pushing the ore into a chute under which trucks on a lower level were loading. Above and beyond the tunnel mouth was the frame cook shack and bunkhouse, while off to the right of the road was the building housing the compressor whose noisy thrashing was constant. Dave caught the high whine of the huge blower fan as they passed its screened mouth and pulled into the level parking area in front of a new metal building housing Tri-State's office.

Everson led the way across the parking lot, palmed open the door and stood aside for Dave to enter. Dave stepped into a sparsely furnished room where three men were leaning over a large drafting table in the corner, their backs to him.

With sudden shock Dave realized that the massive man in the middle, wearing the same tailored suntans, was Chief, the man who had beat him yesterday.

Without breaking stride, Dave walked across the room, put a hand on the man's meaty shoulder, swung him around and drove his fist into his jaw.

Chief crashed against the drafting table and brought it down with him as he fell. Now, one of the startled trio grabbed Dave's arm while Everson, mouth open, simply stared.

Cursing wildly, Chief heaved himself to his feet and started for Dave, just as the second man stepped between them shoving at Chief's chest.

In the midst of this bedlam a door in the side wall opened and Dave saw a blonde woman step into the room.

"Chief!" she said sharply.

Chief subsided instantly and now Dave looked at the girl. She had the palest of hair, done ponytail fashion and she was dressed in charcoal-colored linen Bermuda shorts and white silk shirt. When she looked at him, Dave saw that her eyes were so brown as to be almost black, and now they were dancing with anger. "What's the meaning of this, Scott?" she asked sharply of Everson.

"I don't know, Mrs. Heath," Everson stammered.

She was looking at Dave, and he asked thinly, "Are you Mrs. Heath?"

"Yes."

"My name's Borthen. Now, maybe you know what it's about."

She regarded him with cool appraisal and then said, surprisingly, "I do."

Her glance shuttled to Chief. "It seems you picked on the wrong man," she observed dryly. Now she looked at Dave. "Come into my office, Mr. Borthen." She turned and walked back into the office and Dave glanced at Everson. He saw a faint smile lift the corner of Everson's mouth, but he was still too angry to wonder at it. He tramped past him and into the room where Mrs. Heath was standing by the door.

Dave only saw that the room held files, a metal desk and a dozen wall maps before Mrs. Heath skirted him and seated herself at the desk. They studied each other for a silent moment and Dave was suddenly aware of the fact that he was unshaven, unwashed and still angry.

"Won't you sit down?"

"I'll stand," Dave said coldly.

Mrs. Heath leaned back in the chair, took out a cigarette, lighted it and then said, "Get it off your chest, Mr. Borthen. I can't say I blame you." She smiled disarmingly.

Dave said slowly, "All I want to know is did you give that gorilla his orders?"

"Please sit down," Mrs. Heath begged. "I know you're mad and I'm in the wrong. Frankly I think the whole thing is inexcusable and I'm ashamed." Barely mollified, Dave tramped over to the chair beside the desk and sank into it. For the first time today he could feel his anger ebbing, leaving room now for puzzlement at finding this girl here.

"First, I ought to explain Chief," Mrs. Heath said pleasantly. "I was divorced, Mr. Borthen, from a rich alcoholic by the name of Bill Heath. If you read the gossip columns, you may have heard of him."

"I don't," Dave said brusquely.

"After my divorce, Mr. Heath had the charming

habit of dropping in on me and beating me up. My lawyers hired Chief as a bodyguard. He was an ex-cop in Reno and more than capable of handling my husband. Believe me, he has no connection with the Tri-State companies. He knew that we were anxious to stake this property because we had flown over it and seen your men looking at it. We hadn't finished staking everything we wanted when you surprised us. I think Chief was afraid you'd try to beat us to it."

"Maybe I would have if I'd known, but I didn't," Dave said. "Still I don't like being held while another man beats me up."

"I apologize for that. For beating you to the staking, no."

Dave found himself wondering at her candor.

"I really think we were entitled to it," Mrs. Heath said disarmingly. "We flew a scintillator survey and liked what we found. When we saw your men prospecting it, we knew we had to get in ahead of you."

"Was that just a case of wanting something somebody else wanted?"

Mrs. Heath shook her head. "That can be rather expensive in this game."

Did that mean that Wallen had been wrong, he wondered? He asked bluntly, "Now that you've got it, Mrs. Heath, tell me how good it is."

"Sorry, Mr. Borthen, but that's no business of yours."

Dave grinned faintly and stood up. "You needn't tell me. I can find out for myself."

Mrs. Heath's dark eyebrows rose. "Can you? How?"

"I'll be a neighbor of yours for a while. I'll be watching."

"Neighbor?"

Dave nodded. "I'm leasing the Portland group. We're going to mine it."

Mrs. Heath shrugged. "You're welcome to try." Then she smiled and suddenly her cool propriety vanished. She was a warm, friendly and beautiful person in that moment. Putting out her hand, she said, "I'm glad to hear we'll be neighbors. Maybe we should wish each other luck?"

Dave was conscious of her charm and at the same time he was puzzled by this strange mixture of business cleverness and femininity.

Mrs. Heath came around the desk now, on the way to the door, and Dave had the feeling that this had been Mrs. Heath's victory and not his. Putting her hand on the doorknob, she said, "Now you're out here, wouldn't you like to go through the mine?"

Remembering Everson's words, Dave felt a small disappointment. "I'd like to, but I came out with Everson. I understand he's going back."

"Simple," Mrs. Heath said cheerfully. "I've got another hour's work, and then I'll drive you back to town myself." She opened the door and called, "Harry!"

A young man left his task of repairing a drafting board and came over to them. Mrs. Heath introduced him as Harry Baldwin, junior geologist, and asked him to take Dave through the mine, and she watched them leave.

Then she looked at Everson and said, "Come in, Scott."

When Everson was in the room, Mrs. Heath closed the door and moved around to the desk.

"I just learned some bad news," she said crisply. "Borthen intends to mine the Portland group."

"Oh — oh," Everson said softly.

Mrs. Heath was silent for some moments, gazing out the window, pencil-tapping on the desk.

"I think we can take care of him through Wallen," Mrs. Heath said, "but the most important part can't wait. I want you to go back to town and hunt up Packard right away. Tell him we'll buy the Portland group at his price, provided, of course, that Borthen doesn't exercise his option or renew his lease. If he gets curious about our sudden interest, just say that we want to acquire the Portland because it adjoins our Red Ledge and we're looking for acreage." She hesitated a moment. "You might tell him that date of purchase is effective the very minute Borthen's lease isn't renewed. In other words, sew it up, Scott."

"How high do I go?"

"As high as you have to, and get it signed today. I sent Borthen to have a look at the mine, so he won't be available if Packard gets curious. I'll bring him back to town around six, so get it wrapped up by then, Scott."

"Right," Everson said. "I'm off."

He left the room and now Holly Heath settled

back in her chair, her expression pensive. This Borthen, she thought grimly, was a different package than she had expected. Far from being a meek salesman type, he was handsome, big enough and had nerve enough to tackle Chief. It was a pity that he, like so many personable men, had sawdust in his head. She must remember to tell Chief to watch his behavior.

Now she considered the Portland group situation. Borthen must not be allowed close to Everson's discovery. With his total ignorance of mining, according to Wallen, that shouldn't be difficult. With only a month to go and no money behind him, he couldn't possibly do his required development work before his lease ran out.

Or could he? Holly Heath thought about that for a moment, and suddenly she smiled. She had thought of a way to take care of that.

She reached to the side of the desk and pushed the buzzer. Borthen was taken care of.

When she was just over the Utah line, Abby Channon stopped and put the top up on her second-hand convertible. The blazing sun had beat her dizzy and since the air outside was just as hot as the air inside, there was no advantage in making like a magazine ad, she thought. She hit Joash in the middle of the sweltering afternoon and was immediately entangled in a bedlam of traffic. Besides the car traffic, all the miners who could get away for a town week-end, plus all the miners and prospectors attending the miners' meeting, plus all the ranch people from the surrounding countryside, plus all the tourists like herself, were thronging the half-mile of pavement and the four blocks of stores.

She managed to find a parking spot a couple of blocks from the business district and sat there for minutes wondering what to do. Dave's invitation to come to Joash and his assurance that he would be here today had seemed reasonable a few days ago, but she wondered now how Dave would find her and how best to go about looking for him. She supposed a stroll through the business district was the only answer, and she stepped out into the blazing afternoon and headed for the center of town.

She was hungry, uncomfortable in the heat, and the thought of a milk shake was agonizing. She wondered why she had come to this dusty, baking, God-forsaken spot. The answer, she knew, was that she was sorry she had parted with Dave on such a scolding note. His last memory of her would be that of a nagging and bad-tempered female. Too, she was curious as to what Dave was up to, what the country was like, how he was living and what the future might hold for him.

Soon she was in the slow-moving, roughly dressed crowd that eddied aimlessly on the sidewalks. At the town's single drug store, she found customers lined four deep and had her milk shake standing up. Once on the sidewalk again, she realized there was no place to go. That Dave could find her in this mob seemed an impossibility, but she felt she should give him the chance. She walked the six blocks in the blazing heat, crossed and walked the six blocks back and still no Dave. Her feet hurt, she was tired, thirsty, and temper was edging her. Why were the crowds moving so slowly and always jostling? Why did they come to town in the first place? A child charging against the tide of the crowd brushed against her and disappeared, and she found that he had left a third of his chocolate ice-cream cone on the skirt of her yellow dress.

She had a second milk shake, again standing, and then a kind of desperation seized her. She had to sit down or drop dead. Craftily then, she elbowed through to the counter seat closest to the street, waited patiently for two teenagers to finish their Cokes and when they left, slipped into a seat. From here she could watch the street. And then she began on a series of seven Cokes which took her up to the dinner hour. Still no Dave.

Her temper now was wicked, and she was rehearsing the blast she would give Dave when he came — *if he comes,* she corrected herself angrily. She was watching the street when, through the diminishing auto traffic, she saw a long black convertible of the newest model pull up in front of the bank across the street. While admiring it, she noted with a solid shock that it was Dave behind the wheel. A portion of a blonde head appeared over his shoulder and now Abby stood up on the counter rail to see better. Dave opened the door, slid from under the wheel and then Abby got a full look at the gorgeous blonde who was smiling up at him. They chatted only a few moments, then the blonde drove away, waving good-bye to Dave.

Abby paid her bill, rose and hurried out to the street. Dave was heading south, and now Abby began to run, dodging in and out in the slow highway traffic. A half-block later she caught up with him and called, "Dave!" He halted, turning. When she came even with him, she was breathless and angrier than she could ever remember being.

"Abby!" Dave said, with surprise. "What are you doing here?"

"What am I doing here?" Abby blazed. "I'm being damn well stood up!"

Dave frowned and Abby wondered if she should hit him.

"You said you wouldn't come," Dave said.

"I said nothing of the kind. You said if I decided to come you'd meet me. Like a blundering fool, I did decide."

"Why didn't you let me know?"

"So you've got a phone out at your prospecting camp?"

"Look, baby," Dave said patiently, "this may be out in the back brush, but the U. S. Mails reach here. What's the matter with a postcard?"

It was true, Abby knew, and the knowledge made her all the angrier. She said tartly, "Do they deliver the mail in Cadillac convertibles?"

A look of sudden embarrassment on Dave's face told Abby she had touched a sore spot. "Tell me," she gibed, "does it have a built-in Geiger Counter?"

"I can explain that," Dave said.

"But explain it to me while I'm sitting down," Abby said. "My car's two blocks away. If I get down on my hands and knees I think I can make it." She turned and now Dave fell in beside her. *Everything's wrong,* she thought miserably. *Why do I have to lose my temper?* Forcing contrition upon herself, she said, "I'm sorry, Dave. It's just been hot and crowded and I've been waiting for you all afternoon. Why don't all these people stay home?" She looked at him obliquely and said, "Why didn't I?"

"I'm sorry, too," Dave said. "If I'd known you were coming, I could have made preparations."

"Preparations? What preparations?"

"Well, some place for you to sleep, for instance. It's hard to get a bed in this town."

Oh, Lord, Abby thought, *I've really goofed.*

"Let's eat first and then we'll think about that," Dave said.

At the car Dave got in behind the wheel and they drove back to the business district. At one restaurant they could see customers standing along the wall. At a second they joined the waiting line with prospectors and miners talking over them and around them about today's meeting.

There was no chance to talk, and even if there had been, Abby thought, she was too tired even to try. Half an hour later they got a booth. Only then did Abby discover that the cocktail she had been anticipating to buck her up was only a mirage; she had forgotten that in Utah liquor was sold only in State package stores.

Almost in silence they ate a wretched dinner, and then moved out into the hot evening. The silence between them was a wall, and Abby had the panicky feeling that the man she was with was a stranger and that she didn't care if he was. *This had to stop,* she thought sensibly, as she got into the car. "Can't we go somewhere and talk, Dave?"

"If we can get you a room," Dave said grimly.

Abby knew there was no accusation intended in his words, but there it was, and she felt guilty again, and then angry. In grim silence Dave made the rounds of the motor courts, the one shabby second-floor hotel and then the rooming houses. It took a good hour, and when he returned from the last rooming house, he merely shook his head. It was dark and they were on a quiet side street under the great cottonwoods, and Dave said wearily, "Let's go get a Coke."

Somehow, to Abby this seemed the last indignity. She reached over and turned off the ignition, and then faced Dave. "Dave Borthen, you better talk," she said angrily.

"Name a subject."

"Don't be so damn flip," Abby said hotly. "Where are you living? What are you doing here? Especially what are you doing riding around in a black convertible with a blonde doll? Sure you're prospecting, and I know what for."

In the semidarkness, she saw Dave's jaw set and she didn't care. "Where am I living?" Dave asked ominously. "I'm living on the floor of a shed. What

69

am I doing? Not a damn thing. Who's the blonde doll? Her name is Holly Heath and she owns Tri-State Uranium. That means one operating mine with crazy rich ore and two hundred claims, forty-four of which I thought were Rex Uranium's. Does that answer your questions?"

"She owns your forty-four claims?" Abby asked.

"That's right," Dave said angrily. "Wallen and Hutch sampled the claims and the samples were no good, so they didn't stake. Still they were good enough for Tri-State to stake after we moved out."

"So now you've got what, besides no job?" Abby asked, and she could not keep the malice out of her voice.

"A group of twenty-five lousy claims, if you want to know," Dave said hotly.

"And you'll do what with them?"

"Mine them!" Dave shouted. "That makes you real happy, doesn't it?"

"Fine, fine," Abby said acidly. "The big operator. The president of Rex Uranium. He's retired early in life so he can squire wealthy blondes around the uranium country."

"That was business!"

"Don't shout at me!" Abby shouted. "I'm just a broken-down brunette, but don't talk that way to me."

"Oh, Lord," Dave moaned. "You've driven four hundred miles just to chew me out like you do at home. Why did you bother?"

"I'll never know," Abby said viciously. "Shall we keep looking for a bed?"

Dave started the car and accelerated savagely. He crossed the highway and took a quiet side street, then pulled into an alley and stopped by a shed.

"What's this?" Abby asked coldly.

"This is where my wealthy blonde keeps me," Dave said savagely. He got out and said, "Just sit here and hate me for a while. I'll be back as soon as I can." He was gone a few minutes, then he and a leathery old man appeared in the headlights. They crossed the alley and apparently went up to the back door of the house opposite.

In a few more minutes Dave was back and he approached her side of the car. "This family can give you a room for the night," Dave said coldly. "They don't usually rent rooms, but they're friends of Hutch's." He added, "It's nothing very grand."

"Did I ask for anything grand?" Abby countered waspishly. "All I want is a place to stretch out."

"Come on," Dave said. Abby lifted out her overnight case and when Dave offered to take it she switched it to the other hand. Once out of the headlamps, she stumbled and almost fell. Dave took her arm and she shook off his hand.

They were greeted on the sagging back porch by a slatternly middle-aged woman. Abby managed a smile when Dave said, "This is Mrs. Brogan, Abby."

"Just come along with me, dear," Mrs. Brogan said. A single naked bulb lit the shabby kitchen

71

with its coal stove and cracked linoleum. Beyond the stove Mrs. Brogan turned hard right and entered a room. It was narrow, airless and held a metal cot with a paper-thin mattress. A rickety washstand in the far corner supported a cracked white bowl whose pitcher did not match. On the walls were cut-out calendar illustrations of naked girls of unbelievable symmetry.

Mrs. Brogan said, "I'll get you sheets, dear." She must have caught the look in Abby's face because she said, almost bridling, "I know this ain't much. We keep it for our ranch hands to use when they've got to lay over in town."

"It's very nice," Abby said wanly. She looked up at Dave, hoping that he would take over and make a firm but polite rejection of the room. However, his expression indicated that he thought the whole arrangement satisfactory, and Abby's heart sank to the record low for the day.

"I'll get the sheets," Mrs. Brogan said. She left them standing in the middle of the shabby room, looking at each other.

"Suit you?" Dave asked.

"I said I'd settle for a bed and I will," Abby said ungraciously.

Mrs. Brogan returned with a pair of gray sheets, badly ironed, and pitched them on the cot, then said, "I'll leave you young folks here. I'm going to bed."

They both bid her good night, then looked at each other.

Dave started to say something and Abby raised

her hand. "Tomorrow, Dave, not tonight," she said coldly.

Dave said good night just as coldly, and he did not even try to kiss her, which she wouldn't have allowed anyway.

Abby kicked off her shoes and then sank onto the straight-back chair. It had been a day of sheer unrelieved horror which she supposed would continue through the night. She rose wearily and tried to open the window, but apparently it was painted shut. Returning to the chair, she took out a cigarette and lighted it, noting that the only ashtray in the room was the lid of a coffee can on the washstand, and she was too tired to get it. Slowly she smoked her cigarette down, feeling the sour dregs of anger that would not die. Dave Borthen had lost his mind, she thought. She reviewed what he had told her about losing the claims he was so dependent on. His reason for being out in this fantastic country was now gone and he was on a par with the poorest bum who had come here to seek his fortune. There was no reason for being here — unless this Holly Heath was it. For a wrathful moment Abby wondered if that could be true. Broke and with no prospects in sight and with his job behind him, could Dave be trying to charm himself into the graces of a pretty and rich girl? Abby didn't know. She was too tired to think and this was all so strange as to be something out of a dream.

She looked at the bed and thought, *Well, I might as well face it*. Rising, she snuffed out her cigarette, then shook out the sheets and began to make the bed.

When she lifted the mattress, she saw the bugs scurry for darkness, and with a revulsion that was almost physical sickness she let go the mattress. Then all her anger came back with a rush. She whirled, stepped into her shoes, picked up her overnight case and wrenched open the door. The kitchen was in darkness, but the back door was open. She ran out into the night, stumbling and almost falling. Racing across the back yard, she saw the dim bulk of her car. Reaching it, she yanked open the door, threw in the bag, slipped in under the wheel, turned on the lights and started the car.

The car was just in motion when she saw Dave, clad only in shorts, loom out of the darkness of the shed across the way. He started to run for the car and she stopped, knowing that he might think this was an attempted theft.

"It's me," she said coldly. "I'm going home."

Instead of protesting, Dave said quietly, "Maybe you'd better."

For a stunned second Abby looked at him. "Good-bye, you radioactive schnook," she said viciously, and added, "This is for good, too," before she jammed down the accelerator.

3

Since it was Sunday, Wallen did not want to disturb Mrs. Heath too early, but he knew Dave was impatiently waiting to get started. Besides, hadn't Mrs. Heath told him to let her know where Rex Uranium was going next?

At this hour the cinderblock building housing the telephone exchange was not crowded, and Wallen stepped into a booth and gave the operator the number of Tri-State Exploration.

A man's voice answered and Wallen asked to speak to Mrs. Heath, saying it was important and refusing to give his name. Presently, Mrs. Heath was on the wire. "This is Bates Wallen, Mrs. Heath. I . . ."

"You took your time about calling," Mrs. Heath interrupted.

Puzzled, Bates said, "There's nothing very important to report except that Borthen has decided to mine the Portland group."

"I know that," Mrs. Heath said. "I spent the afternoon with him. Now I want you to listen to this carefully. Where is he now?"

"We're rounding up our equipment before we head out to the Portland."

"All right, go to Borthen and tell him you've been thinking about how strapped Rex Uranium is. Explain to him that he's going to need a road into the Portland group if he's to haul any ore out. Tell him it just cccurred to you that Tri-State will have to put a road into the Red Ledge group for their drill rigs. Suggest to him that he come over and see me this morning and offer to share the cost of the road with me. Have you got that?"

Wallen said he had.

"Now answer some questions," Mrs. Heath said crisply. "Has Rex any assays from the Portland group?"

"Three, all lousy. The highest was seventeen hundredths."

"What was the worst and where is it located?"

"A sample on claim number two assayed five hundredths, and that's in roughly the southeast corner of the group."

"Then start him mining there," Mrs. Heath said. "You've got all that?"

"Sure," Wallen said, "but I can't guarantee he'll be over to see you this morning."

"You weren't asked to," Mrs. Heath said, and hung up.

Swearing under his breath, Wallen came out of the booth. There was no getting close to that dame or even reasoning with her, he thought. On his way across the street to his motel room he wondered what lay behind Mrs. Heath's orders. And why had Borthen seen Mrs. Heath yesterday? Wallen could find no ready answer to his questions and he gave up trying.

Gathering his few belongings from his motel

room, Wallen climbed into the new jeep and drove down the sunlit street to the shed Hutch had directed him to. Pulled up beside it was a big truck loaded with the air compressor and hoses, a water tank, oil drums filled with both gasoline and water since they would be sixty miles from either; a stove and camp gear, the jack hammer or compressed air drill and numberless cartons of canned food. Wallen pulled up beside it and, stepping through the alley door of the shed, he saw no one, but the far door was open and he could hear water splashing.

Walking through the shed, he halted in the doorway. Borthen, stripped to the waist, was shaving without benefit of a mirror; a hose tap on the shed wall was running a stream of cold water at his feet.

Wallen said, "Morning," cheerfully and then, seeing Dave wince, he grinned.

"Hi, Bates. All set to go?" At Bates' nod, Dave said, "Hutch is rounding up his boys. We'll take off when they get here."

Wallen pulled out a cigarette and lighted it, then seated himself against the sunny shed wall and smoked for a moment. He waited until Dave finished his shave and washed his face, and then said in a musing tone, "You know, I got to thinking last night," and looked up at Dave. "Rex hasn't got all the dough in the world, has it?"

"That's an understatement," Dave growled. He scrubbed his face and upper body with a towel.

"Have you figured out what it will cost to get

77

a road into the Portland group?"

"I haven't even seen the Portland group," Dave said.

"There's seven miles of really rugged country between the closest access road and the group. If we're going to haul ore out, we've got to have a road, don't we?"

"If you say so, I guess we do."

"Well, here's what I got to thinking about last night," Wallen said. "Tri-State has the claims next to ours. They're sure to diamond drill that property and they'll need a road to get their drill rigs in." He spread his hands and shrugged. "This may sound crazy, but why don't we go to Tri-State and offer to split the cost of the same road into both properties?"

Dave was reaching for his shirt that was hanging from a nail on the shed wall.

Now his hand stopped and he thought only a second. Then he said, "You're my boy, Bates. You ought to think oftener."

Wallen only grinned, and now Dave shrugged into his shirt, turning this over in his mind. He thought of Mrs. Heath, and both of her apology yesterday and of her wish that their relations might be friendly. If she was sincere, she could prove it by accepting Wallen's suggestion. The only flaw was that Tri-State might not plan to drill immediately, whereas Rex Uranium had to have the road within a matter of days.

"You think I can brace them on Sunday?" Dave asked.

"There's no Sunday in this racket, brother."

"You know who Tri-State is, Bates?" Dave asked. "A very pretty girl about twenty-six by the name of Mrs. Heath."

"No kidding," Wallen said dryly.

"No kidding," Dave answered. "I think I'll call on her now." As he tramped through the shed toward the jeep, Wallen smiled contemptuously.

Dave had no idea where to locate Mrs. Heath on Sunday, but he decided to start with the trailers. Driving toward the trailer lot under the big cottonwoods, he tried to shake off the depression that had been riding him all morning. He could not rid his mind of his savage parting with Abby last night.

In the course of a few days their deep affection for each other seemed to have dried up. Yesterday Abby had been more than unreasonable; she had been downright vicious. All the traits that he had always detested in other women, she had displayed last night, and in spades, he thought. With no warning of her coming he could have done nothing but what he did, and instead of accepting it like a good sport, she had turned on him with unnecessary cruelty. Now, thinking of it, he could not help but compare her tantrum with Holly Heath's handsome and generous conduct only a few hours before.

He pulled into the trailer lot and first knocked on the office door and received no answer. He went to the second trailer and again no one answered the door. Rounding it, he was heading for the third trailer when he glanced toward the back of the lot, and then halted. A grass mat had been spread out in the sun and on one of two canvas lounging chairs Holly Heath lay sprawled in the sun, reading a magazine. She was wearing a black strapless swim suit and sun glasses, and, as Dave started toward her, she swiveled her head.

"Come on over," she called.

When Dave came up, she waved to the other chair, saying, "This is a silly business, but I miss the beach. How are you this morning?"

"Fine," Dave said. He took off his straw hat and said, "I'm afraid I'm out of bounds, though."

"How so?"

"I came to talk a little business and you look like you wanted a vacation from it."

"Half the business in California is done beside a swimming pool," Mrs. Heath said. "I haven't the pool, but I have the chair. Sit down."

Dave accepted her offer and slacked into the other chair. Mrs. Heath's legs were deeply tanned, he noticed, and her trim figure went with the rest of her lean elegance.

"Now, what's this business?"

Without preliminaries, Dave explained that they were setting up camp that day to begin mining the Portland group. A road would soon become a necessity for them. As she knew, they were working on pretty thin capital and it had occurred to him that Rex Uranium and Tri-State could share the cost of the access road to the two properties.

Mrs. Heath listened carefully, and when Dave

was finished, Mrs. Heath said, "Tell me, Mr. Borthen, does Rex Uranium intend to diamond drill the Portland group?"

Dave shook his head in negation.

"That's too bad," Mrs. Heath said. "You see, Tri-State Explorations has a standard policy. We will drill any property that looks good to us for a one-third share of what is turned up. The drilling cost would be ours, of course, and part of the cost would be the road." She paused. "Would Rex be interested in such a deal?"

Dave considered this. With only a month to go before his lease was up, Dave knew that drilling would do them no good, since they would scarcely have time to mine what the drilling found. Suddenly a thought came to him and he voiced it. "Drilling costs would count as development work required in a lease, wouldn't it?"

"Certainly."

Dave felt a faint excitement stir within him. Rex Uranium had a month in which to do fifteen thousand dollars worth of development work or raise money for the cash equivalent. If they were lucky and hit good ore, they could do this. But Wallen's samples had assayed wretchedly. Then why not let Tri-State drill and count their work toward the required development? At the same time Rex could mine as planned, counting on the sale of the ore to raise cash for what the development work did not cover.

"We've got just a month to run, Mrs. Heath, before we have to show fifteen thousand dollars worth of development work. How many dollars worth of drilling would you do in that time?"

"We'd be willing to do half your development — seventy-five hundred dollars worth."

That would leave seventy-five hundred in cash to raise, Dave calculated, and he felt his pulse quicken. The only drawback, and it was a big one, was that a one-third share in the claims to Tri-State would bring bitter protest from his Rex Uranium stockholders.

Now Mrs. Heath's voice cut in on his thoughts, "I think, Mr. Borthen, that Tri-State might make a better deal with Rex Uranium than the usual one. If we're allowed to drill in spots chosen by our Tri-State geologist, we will drill for only a 10 percent share."

Dave frowned. "Why your own geologist?"

Mrs. Heath smiled faintly. "Have you considered, Mr. Borthen . . ."

"Let's make it Dave," Dave said impatiently.

Mrs. Heath gave him that same warm smile. "All right, Dave, my name is Holly."

Dave smiled, too.

"I was about to ask you, Dave, if you had remembered that our Red Ledge group — that's what we call the claims we staked ahead of you — have you thought our Red Ledge group adjoins your Portland group?"

Dave said, "Sure."

"Then the places we chose to drill would be on your Portland group, but just over the boundary from the Red Ledge group. In that way we'll be getting drilling information on our own group, but the drill work will count as your development work."

Dave had a moment of admiration for her shrewdness. He was certain that he could authorize a 10 percent interest in the claims in exchange for drilling and development work without his stockholders protesting.

"That's a deal, Holly," Dave said.

Now Holly Heath rose and said in a businesslike voice, "I'd better get the wheels going. I know you'll want your road as soon as possible."

She extended her hand and Dave accepted it. "Here's to luck in our partnership."

It took Hutch until noon to round up his two miners and the cook. Wallen had gone ahead in the big truck to spot the transfer point where the equipment would be unloaded and hauled the rest of the way into the Portland group by jeep. With the remaining gear Hutch and Dave set out with the company jeep and the crew following.

They drove forty miles south of Joash on the highway before branching off west into the rough access road which took them another twenty miles before they met the big truck returning. A couple of miles farther on into the rolling country timbered with cedar and piñon interspersed with sage flats, they came to the pile of their equipment stacked alongside the road. It would have to be bulled by jeep the rest of the way into the Portland group.

Wallen was sitting on the stacked cases of dynamite when Dave pulled up. Dave directed the cook and the miners to start loading the jeeps and then drew Hutch and Wallen aside.

He explained to them the deal he had made with Tri-State, and Wallen listened closely. When Dave was finished, Wallen gave a low whistle. "You're sure this dame has the right to speak for Tri-State?" Wallen asked.

"The way I read it, she is Tri-State," Dave said. "Why?"

"It's just too good to be true," Wallen said. He paused, the expression on his broad face thoughtful, then he shrugged. "I see her angle though. She's almost drilling her own claims and getting 10 percent of yours while she makes you a present of the development work." He asked curiously, "Who figured out that angle?"

Dave frowned, trying to remember. "Why, both of us I guess."

"You got a great future," Wallen said grinning.

Dave looked at Hutch now to see his reaction, and he saw a look of skepticism on Hutch's face. "What's the matter, Hutch?" he asked.

"What kind of an outfit is this Tri-State anyway?" Hutch asked mildly. "First they kick you and then they kiss you. Which is it?"

Wallen said dryly, "When this is on paper, Hutch, there'll be no mistaking it. It's a kiss."

When the jeep was loaded and the compressor hitched to the new jeep, they took off, Wallen driving the lead jeep. There was no road or trail, and Bates intended to bushwhack his way west until he could pick up the landmark ridge.

As they pushed on, the terrain got rougher. When washes were so deep they could not be skirted, they made dug ways in and out of them, manhandling the compressor, with the aid of both jeeps in tandem. It was wickedly slow and hot going, but by taking advantage of every wash that could be traveled and of any reasonably level terrain, they were close to the group by late afternoon. Far ahead of them to the west was the high red-sandstone ridge, the other side of which, and to the south, they had left only a couple of days ago.

Now the country seemed more familiar to Wallen and he kept looking south and presently put the jeep into a sandy wash. He motioned to Dave to halt his jeep on the bank and when Dave stopped, Wallen called up, "I think this is the wash."

Dave slid down the bank and Wallen said, "Leave the compressor up there until I make sure. There's no sense pulling it out of this if I'm wrong."

Dave swung up on the jeep step, holding to the windshield while Wallen drove on. The banks steepened as Wallen drove slowly down the wash watching the canyon wall on either side. Presently he braked to a stop and pointed to the east wall which seemed to Dave to be no different than the canyon walls they had been traveling past all afternoon.

Wallen pointed and said, "There's where we'll mine."

Dave swung down and Wallen walked over to the rock face. Dave could see marks of Wallen's pick that he had used in sampling. Climbing up the short steep slope of talus, Bates pointed to a faint stain of an orange-brown color in the rough surfaced rock and traced its course for perhaps three feet. Looking down at them, Wallen said, "This stuff assayed the highest of all the samples we took on the group."

He slid down the talus and when he had joined them, Hutch said, "If I'm remembering right, there's a place for the camp a little bit below."

Once more in the jeep, they drove fifty yards down the canyon until Hutch halted them. He scrambled up the sloping canyon wall, Dave at his heels. Dave saw that the ground above was flat and held fair-sized trees and he nodded. Back at the jeep again, Dave said, "Pull out of the wash the next chance you get, Bates. Let's see if we can pull the compressor along the flats."

With Dave standing on the jeep step, they drove on down the canyon.

They all saw the jeep tracks at the same time and Wallen halted. Tire marks came down the bank, crossed the wash and climbed out. For a surprised moment no one spoke. Then Dave swung down, moved over to the bank and examined the tracks. "Those are fresh."

He looked at Bates and pointed to the right bank. "Pull up and let's see who the visitor is. Are we still on the Portland group?"

Bates only nodded. He set the jeep in low and swung up the right bank in the tracks of the other jeep. Pulling up on the flats, Wallen followed the jeep tracks around the clump of cedar and braked abruptly. There ahead of them, sitting in a Tri-State jeep in the sparse shade of a piñon, his new straw hat shoved on the back of his head, sat Chief. For a puzzled moment Dave looked at him. Then he stepped down and turned off the jeep engine.

"Well, well, the money boys," Chief said.

Dave felt the old anger rising, and he tramped over to Tri-State's jeep, hearing Wallen and Hutch following him. Hauling up beside Chief's massive bulk, Dave asked coldly, "What are you doing here?"

"Just sitting, Jack, just sitting," Chief said.

His contemptuous tone of voice told Dave that their meeting yesterday had changed nothing as far as Chief was concerned. He remembered Holly Heath's words. *Believe me, Chief has no connection with Tri-State.* Dave looked at Chief's face, which was overlaid with an insufferable arrogance, and he said, "Right back at you, Chief. You're on claims I lease and you're trespassing. Get off."

"I like it here, Jack," Chief said calmly.

Dave felt his anger pushing him. "I got drop-kicked off Tri-State claims. How'd you like to get tossed off these?"

Chief looked at him thoughtfully, "I wouldn't try it, Jack. Mrs. Heath might object. Besides I've got a couple of boys out in the back brush looking for drill spots."

The gall of the man was like a goad; Dave remembered how Chief had directed the Tri-State staker to hold the gun on Hutch while Chief worked him over. He said now, "The boys can stay in the back brush, Chief. You get out."

"Tut, tut," Chief said disdainfully. "Think of Mrs. Heath."

But the rising anger in Dave pushed past that warning. He said, "These are claims leased to Rex Uranium. I told you to get off."

Chief looked at him with cold appraisal. "If you can cut the mustard, Jack, throw me off."

Dave reached out, balled Chief's shirt front in his big fists, and yanked him sideways out of the jeep. In the astonished second that it took Chief to comprehend what was happening, the act was done, and he found himself lying at Dave's feet. He scrambled to his knees, already reaching inside his shirt, and then he came erect, backed up and there was a snubnosed Police Positive in his hand. "That was a mistake," he said ominously.

Dave's wrath was at full tide now, and he began to walk slowly toward Chief. "Put that down," he said quietly, and he kept walking.

Chief backed up a step, his eyes chill. "You damn fool, I'll shoot."

Dave's voice grew colder. "You won't shoot. You're Mrs. Heath's sheep dog, but you're not guarding her now. You can't even pull self-defense, Chief. These are my witnesses, not yours," and he was still walking.

Chief backed up another step and Dave saw he had scored. It showed on Chief's face, and Chief knew it showed, and for the first time Dave saw real anger mount in his policeman's eyes.

"You like it rough, you'll get it rough," Chief said. With a flick of his wrist, he flipped his gun aside and charged.

Dave charged too, but even as he was moving he saw that Chief was diving at his knees in a risky attempt to get him down. Dave bent his legs as if to drop and Chief crashed into the point of his knees. The move stopped Chief as if he had been brought up against a stone wall, and Dave heard the pained explosion of breath escape from Chief's chest.

Half over him now, Dave reached down and seized the thick shock of black hair, yanked Chief's head back and drove a sledging fist into his cheek, before he came erect and stepped away. Chief heaved his big hulk to his knees and Dave moved in, lifting a knee solidly into his face. The force of the blow straightened Chief's back and sent him sprawling on his side with his back to Dave. Instinctively he rolled over and fought to get on his feet, and now Dave saw that his mouth was open, gasping for air, and that his nose was bleeding. Dave lunged in now, slugging savagely before Chief could come fully erect. Like a massive animal, ponderous and wounded, Chief stood his ground, bracing himself against any retreat. He fought blindly now, his arms sledging in short arcs, trying to draw Dave to him.

In a saner moment Dave would have stood away, knowing that Chief's massive shoulders and arms held the strength to crush him, but total rage was in him now. He stood his ground, rolling wicked, rocketing punches inside Chief's arms into his big belly, and this for perhaps six furious seconds, until a blind and panicked swipe from Chief's forearm caught him alongside the ear. It staggered him back against the Tri-State jeep, and he felt a knifing pain across the small of the back as the tailgate caught him.

Chief was half bent over now, his arms wrapped around his middle, sucking in great gusts of air. In his eyes was a raw hatred, and something else, too, which Dave knew was fear.

Dave didn't pause. He ran at Chief, and the bigger man half turned his shoulder to take the expected impact. Again Dave reached out with his left hand and buried his fist in Chief's hair and yanked. Then with his right hand he drove the butt of his palm under Chief's square jaw. Chief's head snapped back as if his neck were broken and his knees simply dissolved under his weight. He fell against Dave, and Dave backed off, letting him fall to the ground on his face.

Slowly then, Dave drew his arm across his face, and only then saw Wallen and Hutch silently watching him.

Dave stood panting for perhaps ten seconds in the electric afternoon silence, and then he said, "Throw him in his jeep."

Hutch and Bates moved over to Chief and picked

him up. Together they had to strain to hoist his inert hulk into the jeep's carryall. Now Dave said, "Drive him to the edge of our claims, Bates. I don't care where."

Wallen gave him a look of surprise and disapproval, then slipped into the seat, started the jeep and drove it past the other two jeeps.

Hutch wordlessly turned toward the new jeep, lifted out a canteen, came over to Dave as he unscrewed the top and handed the canteen to Dave. Dave fought to slow his breathing so that he could drink, and in that moment he and Hutch looked at each other.

"I wish it was whiskey," Hutch said. "You earned it."

Dave heard the jeep motor die and then Wallen came tramping back to where the two of them stood in the blazing sunlight. Wallen's face, Dave saw, was sulky and scared as Wallen halted in front of him.

"That was a real short partnership with Tri-State, wasn't it?"

Dave ignored this, taking a drink of water.

"You shouldn't have done it, Dave," Wallen said, a heavy reproof in his voice.

"Well, I did it," Dave said flatly.

"There goes your road, and there goes your drilling."

"Maybe." Dave looked at him, the dregs of anger still in his eyes. "Maybe you can mine uranium on your knees, Bates, but I can't. I won't even try."

"That goes double for me," Hutch said quietly.

Wallen shrugged. "Not me. I'd put up with him. I'd even have made friends with him." There was a kind of anger in his gesture as he shrugged again. "Well, what do we do now?"

"Just what we started out to do," Dave said sharply. "Set up our camp."

Drs. Channon and Busbee shared a common reception room in a tiny modern clinic that was one of Ute City's newest buildings. The window of the reception room looked out across a napkin-size piece of lawn onto a broad tree-shaded residential block.

From her reception desk, Abby had learned to watch the street to sort out her father's and Dr. Busbee's patients before they entered, and to make a bet with herself as to which doctor a stranger would choose. But these past two weeks she had found herself watching for something else — the mailman.

By the end of the week, with not so much as a postcard from Dave, the self-righteous feeling that had been warming her began to turn chill. From feeling that she had been ignored and treated outrageously, she felt that perhaps, just perhaps, she had acted hastily in leaving Joash so abruptly. Once the first doubt entered her mind, the door was opened and a hundred doubts followed, so that when Thursday's mail was barren and Friday's too, she was in a state of controlled panic.

She stacked the 4 o'clock mail delivery, empty

of word from Dave, on the desk and, because the room was full of people who had nothing to look at but each other and her, she opened her appointment book and pretended to study it in stony-faced silence. Dave, she was convinced now, was not going to make up. All the things she had said to him last week-end came back in bitter memory, and they shocked her with their violence.

The phone rang and she answered automatically. She escorted a number of people to each doctor's consultation room, a frozen smile of politeness on her face. Until six she typed correspondence, made appointments, chatted with the waiting patients and discreetly gossiped, and later she could not remember a person she had spoken to or what she had said or typed.

Dr. Busbee's consultation room light was off, which meant he had left by the back door, and now Mrs. Erlin, Dr. Channon's last patient came out, followed by Eva, his nurse; both said good night and hurried through the reception room to the street. This was what Abby was waiting for and she entered her father's consultation room. Dr. Channon, in white coat, was seated at a bleak modern desk in the corner writing something. At Abby's entrance, he looked up and she saw how tired his fleshy, benign face seemed. Dr. Channon returned to his writing, saying, "What are you hanging around for?"

Abby switched off the overhead fluorescent lamp and settled into a comfortable chair facing the desk out of the light of the lamp. She said wryly, "I've come to consult you, doctor." She shook loose a cigarette from the pack she was carrying in her skirt pocket and put her lighter to it. Her hand was shaking so that the flame wavered and she looked across to see her father regarding her curiously.

"You don't have to recite the symptoms," Dr. Channon said.

Abby said, relieved, "I'm leaving you, Pa."

Dr. Channon leaned back in his chair. "For where?"

"Dave."

"It's about time," Dr. Channon said. "Why didn't you go with him?"

"No scolding, please," Abby said. She was silent a moment. "We had a terrible row last week-end. He's mixed up with some woman over there who's loaded with money, and . . ."

"Nonsense," Dr. Channon cut in.

"I was just reciting my fears, Pa," she said bitterly, "but if you want the facts, here they are. He lost those forty-four claims he was counting on. I think he's close to broke. The closer he is, the more stubborn he is. He" — here Abby spread her hands imploring — "he just needs me, Pa, and I ratted on him."

"You don't need him?"

"Like crazy. That's why I think I'll go out there."

"Then get going," Dr. Channon said, and then he observed quietly, "You won't believe it, Abby, but humility becomes you."

On this trip Abby was wiser than before. Remembering the name of a Joash tourist court, she wired ahead so that a room was awaiting her when she arrived Sunday evening. Early Monday morning she entered the U. S. Employment Office located in a dingy unused store building on one of Joash's side streets. An ancient store counter stood before her and behind it were a couple of card tables with chairs for interview purposes and the usual government files, desk and typewriter.

A pale young man in glasses greeted her, and Abby announced she was looking for a job as stenographer-secretary. This announcement brought a stirring of skeptical interest in the young man's eyes and he invited her to take a chair at one of the card tables behind the counter. Patiently, then, he asked her experience, training, her typing speed and whether she could take dictation. At each of Abby's answers he showed a keener interest.

Presently he rose and went over to the files and came back with a sheet of paper. "Miss Channon, I don't know if you understand the situation here. Only a few of the biggest companies want to hire girls on a permanent basis. Is that what you want?"

"Just a steady job," Abby said.

The man smiled cynically. "That's what they all say until they find that by working as a public stenographer they can make twice the money a big company will pay them. Then they quit. You see the dozens of mining companies around here haven't enough secretarial work for a full-time girl. They'd rather pay a premium to a public stenographer for part-time work."

"That's not for me," Abby said firmly. "I want a nine to five job in one place."

The clerk nodded happily. "One more thing. Please understand it's hard to find a place to live here and there's nothing to do except go to movies you've probably seen. As for men, they're all out hunting uranium."

You're telling me, Abby thought. The interviewer handed a sheet of paper to her, saying, "Here are four companies wanting permanent secretary-typists. Take your choice."

Abby looked at the four names, which meant nothing to her. She was about to hand it back when one of the names nudged her memory. Tri-State Exploration. For a moment she wondered why it seemed familiar. Then it came to her. Hadn't Dave said the blonde doll in the black convertible owned Tri-State Uranium?

For a moment Abby hesitated. If she got a job with Tri-State, would Dave think she was spying on him? *Damn right he will,* she thought grimly. Well, why not? *If I've got competition I might as well study it.* She made her decision then.

Abby looked up at the interviewer. "Eenie, meenie, minie, mo," she said and put her finger on Tri-State. "Let's see what I drew. Tri-State Explorations?"

"Very good." The young man got a card from the desk, filled it out, signed it, gave it to her and directed her to the Tri-State lot.

Outside Abby began to wonder. Would this

move merely heap fuel on Dave's anger? She couldn't pretend to him she hadn't known what she was doing, and the first time she saw Dave the news would out. Let it, she thought. If she lost this job she could always be a public stenographer.

A little after 9 o'clock she drove into the Tri-State lot. Under one of the cottonwoods was a slick, newly washed, black convertible, and Abby parked her shabby convertible by it. She looked at the five trailers with bewilderment. She had expected a building of some sort, however temporary, but not this. Hesitantly, then, she approached the biggest trailer beside the radio mast and knocked on the door. A short grizzled man answered the door, and Abby said, "Is this the Tri-State Explorations' office?"

Everson nodded.

Abby said, "The employment office sent me out here saying you wanted a secretary-typist."

Everson smiled. "Come in, come in, young lady. That we do."

Abby stepped into the trailer and immediately a look of wonder came into her face. This was like the plushest kind of city office with twice the room she expected. At one of the two desks in the rear, a stenographer was silently typing. Beyond her a man with earphones sat at a huge radio from which subdued voices were coming. Maps were thumbtacked to the trailer walls and there was even a small bar opposite the lounge.

Everson said, "Go along to the free desk. We'll

see what you can do."

Abby went back to the empty desk, a little awed by the impersonal speed with which this was all happening. There was no chatting here, but all business.

There was a pad and pencil on the desk and as soon as she was seated and had picked them up, Everson began reading what Abby was later to identify as a claim description. It was complicated and held terms which were new to Abby. Besides, Everson was purposely reading fast, but not so fast that Abby couldn't get it.

When Everson finished, he said, "Type it, please."

Abby squared herself to the typewriter, propped open her book and began to type. Again she knew that Everson had purposely picked a difficult demonstration piece. She had typed five lines effortlessly when Everson reached over, ripped out the sheet and scanned her work. Only then did Everson smile. He bowed, mockingly and said, "You're a real pro, Miss . . ."

"Channon. Abby Channon."

"Miss Channon, what have we done to deserve you?"

Abby smiled with pleasure.

"My name is Scott Everson. Come up front and tell me about yourself. Incidentally," he added, "you're hired. We'll pay you whatever you're worth and right now you're worth a mint to us." Everson took her elbow and stopped at the second desk.

"Joyce, this is Miss Channon. Joyce Reddish."

Abby said hello to the attractive blonde girl who stopped her typing long enough to grin and say, "Hi."

Abby walked back to the red lounge and seated herself. She felt a tingle of pleasure. Once she had proved herself, this man turned out to be human after all. Everson sat down opposite her, and offered her a cigarette which she accepted along with a light. "Now," Everson began, "I want you to understand everything about this job. In the first place we provide a trailer for you to live in. You'll have it to yourself. There is a kitchen and air-conditioning. I think you'll find it more attractive than most of the accommodations in town."

"May I look around before I decide?"

Everson smiled. "Sorry. That's part of the job. We like our personnel right here and for a good reason, Miss Channon. We're in a multimillion-dollar business and this is a boom camp. Gossip, a wrong word dropped unknowingly, and our plans are shot. We like to think by giving you pleasant living quarters we remove the temptation of being indiscreet."

Abby looked at him carefully. "A mink-lined jail, you mean?"

Everson smiled tolerantly. "Not at all. You're free to come and go as you like. It's just that we want this to be more pleasant than coming and going for you."

Abby nodded dubiously.

"This question may seem impertinent, Miss

Channon, but please answer it. Believe me, it figures. Why are you here?"

Abby didn't hesitate a second. "To be close to the man I'm going to marry."

"And what is his business?"

Abby laughed. "Right now he's out somewhere prospecting. Isn't everybody?"

Everson grinned. "Quite right. I ask because most girls stay here only if they have a good reason to stay here. Your reason is the same as Joyce's."

Abby felt relieved. If he had asked her the name of her man and his organization it might have made a difference, but he hadn't.

"As to salary," Everson continued, "you'll start at three hundred a month. That's provisional, of course. If you're as good as you seem to be, I'm sure Mrs. Heath will pay you more." He paused. "Mrs. Heath," he said in reverential tones, "is majority stockholder of both Tri-State Uranium and Tri-State Explorations."

Abby thought she should be properly surprised, so she said, "A woman?"

"A very capable woman," Everson said crisply, "and a most charming person."

I'll bet, Abby thought.

Now Everson said, concluding the conversation, "As soon as you're settled, you can go to work. May I help you move?"

"My bags are in the car," Abby said, rising.

She led the way out to her convertible and Everson unloaded her bags, carrying them to the third trailer. Entering, Abby saw that Everson hadn't exaggerated. There was a three-quarter bed, pastel green walls with matching rug and a folding screen which shut off the bed from the living area which held a sofa and two chairs of modern design and a folding table against the wall.

Putting down her bags, Everson said, "Take your time, Miss Channon. We've lived this long without you, a little while longer won't matter."

He left and Abby unpacked her bags and hung up her clothes and, oddly enough, she found herself humming. She had a notion that she had walked into something special in this job, but she couldn't be sure until she met Mrs. Heath. Maybe Mrs. Heath was the reason the hired help was tendered this loving care. Finished, she left her trailer, walked over and entered the office trailer. As she stepped inside, she saw Everson seated by a stunning-looking blonde woman in her late twenties whom Abby recognized instantly by her pale hair. Everson rose and said, "Mrs. Heath, this is Abby Channon, our new secretary, and a crackerjack one."

Mrs. Heath's dark eyes appraised Abby briefly and at the same time she held out her hand. "Welcome, Miss Channon," Holly Heath said cordially, and then she added, "Scott didn't tell me you were so pretty."

Abby accepted her hand and said with the same candor, "He didn't tell me you were, either."

Somehow this caught Holly Heath off guard and she colored a little. "I hope you'll like us," she added simply. At the same time there was unmistakable dismissal in her tone and it was Abby's turn to feel embarrassment. She smiled faintly and went to her desk.

Everson followed and gave her two corrected leases to type out, and Abby set to work, her back to Joyce. In spite of her resolution not to be impressed by Mrs. Heath, Abby could not help herself. That much beauty should not go with that much money, she thought, remembering Everson's reference to this being a multimillion-dollar business. But what impressed Abby, and chilled her, too, were Holly Heath's eyes. *On an Arabian slave dealer they'd look good,* Abby thought, and she wondered why she resented them so much. Soon she could hear Mrs. Heath's voice above the almost silent clicking of the typewriters, and it was as expressionless as any banker's.

Everson came and went between the lounge and the radio over which a pimply-faced young man hovered.

Abby was typing swiftly when she was aware of a new voice in the conversation. She looked up to see a huge man standing just inside the doorway, a straw hat in his meaty fist. Covering his entire nose and extending to his bruised cheeks was a bandage. His big jaw was swollen lopsidedly and his left arm was in a sling over which his coat was buttoned. Everyone in the trailer had ceased work and was looking at him, and now Mrs. Heath's cold voice cut into the silence. "Did they give you a good room, Chief?"

"The room was good, but the food was lousy,"

Chief said. He stepped into the room as far as the lounge and added, "Doc said not to talk much or my jaw would go out again." He shook his head. "I don't heal quick any more."

Abby turned to regard her work, thinking this should be none of her business, but she noticed Joyce watching attentively.

"You won't need to talk, Chief," Mrs. Heath said. "May I have that envelope, Scott?"

Everson handed her an envelope which she extended across the table to the man she called Chief. He reached out and accepted it frowning.

"That's severance pay, Chief, plus a one-way plane ticket to Las Vegas from Salt Lake. Perez will wait until you've packed and then he'll drive you in."

Abby stole a glance at the big man. His bandages and bruises could not hide his look of consternation. "You mean I'm fired?" he asked then.

"I do."

"But what did I do?"

"You are not a bodyguard, Chief," Mrs. Heath said in the voice Abby was learning to hate. "You can't even guard your own body."

"But three of them . . ."

"It's no good, Chief. There was only one. You shouldn't have been out there and you should have left when he told you to leave. You shouldn't have pulled a gun and you shouldn't have fought — or shall I say tried to fight." The contempt in her voice was undisguised.

Chief Buford's policeman's eyes were unreadable. He was silent a moment and then said, "Your lawyers hired me, Mrs. Heath."

"And I hire my lawyers," Mrs. Heath said tartly. "This was all settled with them, Chief, while you were in the hospital. I don't need you, and I'm beginning to think I never did."

Chief was silent a long moment regarding her, and then he said, "What's the real reason, Mrs. Heath? You like the guy, don't you?"

Mrs. Heath's voice had never seemed colder as she said, with Abby listening, "The real reason, Chief, is that I'm involved with Rex Uranium to the tune of several hundred thousand dollars. My relations with them are too important to me to allow you to wreck them."

It was then Abby resumed typing, and furiously.

4

Standing on the pile of waste rock on one side of the tunnel, Dave waited impatiently for the powder fumes to disperse and the rock dust to settle. It was past five and the crew had gone back to camp, leaving Dave and Wallen to shoot off the day's second round.

"Okay?" Dave asked impatiently.

"Let's go," Wallen said. They both struck their carbide lamps alight, fitted them into the slots of their hard hats, picked up a shovel apiece and Dave led off into the tunnel. The dust was still thick and the powder fumes strong, but it was only one more annoyance in two weeks of worse ones, and Dave tramped the thirty feet to the face. Once there, he and Wallen climbed over the pile of new rock, mucked out that which remained against the face, and then by the light of their lamps carefully began to study the gray, newly exposed rock of the face.

Studying it, Dave felt his spirits sink. After shooting the first round today, the lens had pinched down from yesterday's two feet to one foot. And now Dave saw that it had pinched out entirely.

Turning his head to put his light on Wallen, he saw the discouragement in Bates' face.

"She's gone," Bates said tonelessly.

"All right, let's knock it off." Dave's tone was one of utter discouragement. He turned and clambered over the pile of rock, and already his head was beginning to ache from the powder fumes. Once outside, he halted, drew out a cigarette and offered one to Bates who declined. Wearily Dave took off his hat and blew out his lamp, and then said to Bates, "You go on. I'll be over later."

Wallen stepped over the track, passed the ore car and, holding on to the wooden ore bin, dropped down to the sandy canyon floor and headed toward camp.

Bone weary, Dave moved over to the ore car and leaned on it. He scrubbed his face tiredly with a sore palm as if trying to rub away the lines of gloom and discouragement. Not counting the three days it took them to set up the camp and to bull in a rental air compressor for the pneumatic drill, water tank, drill steel, hoses, powder, fuse and caps, lengths of eight-pound rail and the mine car, they had been mining almost two weeks. The results had been uniformly discouraging and right now they were appalling. There remained thirteen days before his lease was up.

Dave regarded the tunnel with bitterness now, almost hating it. Three times in the past week Hutch had driven into Joash with samples of ore they had mined that day, and each time he had returned with an assay that showed their ore was running less than fourteen hundredths U_8O_8. *Not even wages*, Dave thought now.

Tomorrow, he knew, their first round would

be wasted in blasting out the country rock in an effort to pick up the ore body again. With two weeks to go before Rex Uranium's lease was up, Dave knew there was no way of mining and shipping enough ore to pay for the development work that Tri-State couldn't do. True, Tri-State's drill camp, three hundred yards up the wash from Rex's camp, had been set up for ten days, and three drills had been moved onto the Portland group and were operating. With all this help, plus the road Tri-State had put in, counting toward his development, Dave knew that the thousands of dollars more which they would require must come from the ore, and he was not getting it.

Straightening, he flipped away his cigarette and wearily slid down past the half-filled ore bin to the canyon floor. Tramping up the wash, Dave again felt a quiet rage at his own helplessness and ignorance. Since they'd been mining he had learned to manhandle the jack hammer, load and blast a round, and hand sort ore as well as the next man, but his ignorance of geology appalled him. He knew only too well, and bitterly, that he was at Wallen's mercy. With time running out on them, were they mining in the right place? The answer to that was that he didn't know. At night by the light of the gasoline lantern, he had studied Bates' books on geology, pestering Wallen with questions until Wallen, out of self-defense, went to bed. *But I'm only kidding myself,* he thought. He knew that a man has not learned an exacting profession in a week, or a month, or even a year.

As he cut across the wash out of the hot sun to pick up the shade of the bank, the question that had been nagging him for days now floated to the top of his mind. Abruptly then, thinking of days of discouraging progress, he came to his decision.

Clinging to the wash, he passed Rex Uranium's camp which consisted of a single wall tent, a stove set up outdoors and a rough table which the cook had knocked together from lumber left over from constructing the ore bin. Wallen was washing up and the two miners Hutch had obtained for him were stretched out on the ground awaiting supper. Dave passed them, heading for the drill camp up the wash. The mere fact that he had come to a decision lifted his spirits.

Climbing out of the wash, he saw the drill camp ahead of him. Smoke was coming from the chimney of the commissary trailer which was the biggest of the five trailers which housed the three drill crews. A tall guyed radio mast rose beside it. A stubby tank truck was parked alongside the thousand-gallon aluminum-painted water tank, its pump thrashing noisily as the water was transferred. Dave waved to the driver, passed through a tangled clutter of timbers, cables, oil drums and core boxes that littered the ground, and finally achieved the bulldozed road which headed up over the ridge.

He could hear the diesel engine of the nearest drill rig thrashing away, and he knew that Everson would be somewhere around. Achieving the top of the ridge, Dave saw the first drill rig in the hollow below him. Everson was talking to one of the three-man crew, and as Dave tramped down the hill, he saw Everson turn to look at him. This was the second time he had seen Everson since the fight with Chief Buford. The first time was on Wednesday when Everson, with Tri-State's papers of agreement in his hand, had come over to Rex Uranium's camp one evening for Dave's signature. He had been friendly, but reserved, and no mention had been made of Mrs. Heath's displeasure over Chief's treatment. It was as if the fight had never taken place.

As Dave approached, Everson stepped away from the cab and the two-and-one-half-ton truck which held the diesel-powered drill. Two of the crew who were leaning on the towering drill mast were watching the drill and the wet slush oozing up around it.

Dave nodded in a friendly enough fashion, and Everson nodded, too. "How's it going?" Dave asked.

Everson grimaced. "Come and look." He went over to the truck's cab, lifted the Geiger Counter from the seat, and then moved over to the open core box lying by the rig. This was an oblong, six-foot wooden box with grooved racks which held the labeled cores the diamond drill disgorged. The box was almost full of cores and now Everson switched on the Geiger Counter and knelt over the box. He moved the probe up and down close over the cores, and watching the Geiger's dial, Dave saw that the hand barely moved. That meant only a trace of radioactivity. When Everson rose, Dave said, "How deep are you?"

"We lost a drill yesterday, so we're only three sixty here. The other two are over four hundred."

The two men looked at each other questioningly, and Dave felt his discouragement deepen. He shifted a little so that the late sun, still hot, would be out of his eyes and he could watch Everson. Gauging Everson's temper, he thought the older man seemed friendly enough and he decided to put his question. "Has Mrs. Heath told you to leave us alone, Everson?"

A look of surprise came into Everson's face. "Leave you alone? I don't know what you mean."

"I mean you've dropped in on us once and that's all."

Everson still looked bewildered. "Why, I have my job to do, which is directing this drilling."

"Have you read my agreement with Tri-State?"

"I helped draw it up."

"Doesn't it read that Tri-State, in exchange for drilling and road work, gets 10 percent of anything found on the Portland group of claims?"

"Certainly."

"Has it occurred to you," Dave persisted, "that you're getting 10 percent of what Rex is mining right now?"

"That goes without saying."

"Then if we're together on these claims, what we're turning out should interest you people, shouldn't it?"

Everson nodded cautiously, and then his eyes

turned shrewd, as if he at last had spotted the joker in what Dave was about to say.

"Do you think we're mining in the right place?" Dave went on.

Everson shrugged. "That's not for me to say."

"It's for you to say, if you will," Dave said bluntly.

"What are you getting at, Borthen?"

"We're mining lousy stuff," Dave said. "The ore body pinched out today and if lucky we'll pick it up tomorrow, but it'll still be lousy stuff. You've guessed that already, haven't you?"

Everson nodded.

"All right," Dave went on. "We haven't the dough to drill. We can't ask you because we have no say in your choice of drill spots. But you can help us and Tri-State at the same time without drilling."

"How's that?"

"We're mining on Wallen's knowledge of geology, plus what his grab samples show. I'd rather mine on your knowledge of geology and no samples."

Everson looked at him a long moment. "I'm perfectly willing, but is Wallen?"

"The hell with Wallen," Dave said bluntly, and he tried to keep the exasperation out of his voice.

"How long does your lease run? Two weeks more, isn't it?"

Dave nodded.

"It would take one of those weeks for a preliminary geologic survey and sample job. Even then I could be wrong. If I were always right, I wouldn't be working for Tri-State."

"I know that. All I'm asking for is your educated guess, and your guess has more education than Wallen's."

"I'd have to clear this with Mrs. Heath," Everson said cautiously. "I'd suggest you clear it with Wallen."

"You're in radio contact with her, aren't you?" Dave said. At Everson's nod, he added, "Then clear it. As for Wallen, he'll never know it happened. When you're in a mine you don't see much," Dave added dryly.

"I don't like that," Everson said.

"Professional courtesy?"

Everson nodded, and Dave said, "You let me handle the courtesy. We'll shoot two rounds tomorrow. If we pick up the ore body and it doesn't look better, I'm pulling off the crew. I'd like to be able to move them to your spot."

"You mean I get tomorrow to pull this out of the hat?" Everson asked.

"That's what I'd like."

Everson looked at Dave a moment. "You have a touching faith," he observed.

"Not me," Dave said grimly. "I just got desperation. Is it a deal?"

Dave talked a few minutes longer, arranging for the tank truck to deliver water to the Rex Uranium tank, and then he left. Tramping back to camp, he wondered if he'd been a fool. No man, not even Everson, could in a day's time be expected to point to an exact area and say, "Dig here and you'll find a good grade of uranium ore." Still, if Everson got Mrs. Heath's consent, he would be accepting the wildest kind of challenge, one that went against the cautious grain of every trained geologist. In short, Everson would be forced to play his hunch and Dave believed his hunch would prove better than Wallen's lazy reconnaissance.

The crew had already eaten when Dave returned to camp. The cook was wiping the rough table; the chairs for it were upended empty dynamite boxes. The two miners Hutch had hired, both elderly men, had finished eating and were stretched out in the shade of the near piñon. Only Wallen remained at the table, and Hutch had not yet shown up from town.

Dave took his plate over to the stove which was a converted fifty-gallon oil drum with eight feet of guyed stove pipe in which there was a chimney oven.

The cook, a Spanish-American who knew a bare two dozen words of English, helped him to a hot stew, biscuits and potatoes, and Dave tramped back to the table where Wallen was moodily smoking.

"You don't look happy," Dave observed as he began to eat.

"Neither do you," Wallen said sullenly.

"Cheer up, Bates. With any luck, you've only got one more day of it."

"What does that mean?"

"If the assay Hutch brings in tonight isn't better than the others, here's what I'm doing. We'll shoot off two rounds tomorrow. If we don't pick up the ore body again, or if it isn't twice as wide as what we've been mining, we're pulling out."

"For where?" A kind of alarm was in Bates' broad face, and Dave wondered why.

Dave shrugged, and Bates said solemnly, "According to the samples, we're mining the highest grade stuff now."

"Then let's jump to the next spot you sampled."

"That's foolish."

Dave looked at him. "It's foolish mining where we are."

"But if it's the best . . ."

"If it doesn't improve tomorrow, we're moving," Dave interrupted flatly.

Wallen finished his coffee and rose. "You're the boss," he said resignedly. Dave watched him as he moved over to the wash and strolled off toward the drill camp. Rex Uranium's crew this past week had formed the habit of dropping in after supper on the drill crew for a game of cards or talk. So long as there was no whiskey involved, Dave didn't care; it gave them some relaxation after a long day.

The sun was fully down and twilight beginning as Dave, finished with his lonely meal, got his second cup of coffee and lighted a cigarette. He was heading back for the table when, above the soft clatter of the cook washing dishes, he picked up the sound of a jeep.

In a few minutes Hutch pulled into camp, parked beside the tent, and stepped out.

In his right hand he held an envelope and in his other a bulging flour sack.

Approaching, Hutch's seamed face was inscrutable. He said, "This what you want, Dave?" and handed him the envelope.

Dave ripped open the envelope and pulled out the assay of yesterday's sample. It was twelve hundredths, just a little worse than the assay of the day before.

Unsurprised, Dave threw the envelope on the table and watched Hutch dump out the camp mail on the table. Listlessly, then, Dave helped him sort the mail. There was a letter from Rex Uranium's treasurer in Ute City that would contain a check for one thousand dollars, which was the July stockholders' assessment with which Dave could meet the payroll. He leafed through the other mail, all unimportant, until he came to a letter bearing the printed return address of Tri-State Explorations.

Only faintly curious, Dave opened the letter, wondering if this were more business about the agreement.

The first words he read were "Dear Dave" in Abby's handwriting.

With a sense of shock, he glanced down at the signature and saw it was Abby's. For a bewildered moment Dave simply stared at the Tri-State letterhead and at the greeting, trying to associate Abby with Tri-State. Then he read the note which said,

"I've got to see you. I'll be at the Manhattan road-house between seven and eleven every night until you come. The Manhattan is thirty miles south of Joash and you pass it on the state highway on your way to town. Abby."

Dave read and reread it and it still made no sense whatever. He saw the Tri-State envelope was postmarked Joash as of yesterday's date. Then he looked carefully again at the handwriting. Unmistakably it was Abby's.

For baffled minutes Dave tried to bring some plausibility to the fact that Abby was writing on Tri-State stationery, and he could not. Pocketing the letter, he waited until Hutch brought his plate to the table and then asked, "How's the gas in the jeep, Hutch?"

"Over half full."

"I think I'll take a ride."

"I'll help you unload."

Dave rose, putting his hand on Hutch's shoulder. "Sit down and eat."

He moved over to the jeep, unloaded the groceries and gear Hutch had brought from town, and then drove over to the bulldozed road to the access highway which joined the state highway some twenty miles to the northeast.

As he drove, he found that he was facing this appointment with a vast reluctance. In the past two weeks, with no word from Abby, he had begun to accept the fact that they were through. What he was doing only angered her, and she had only contempt for it. Far from apologizing, she hadn't

116

even written. Apparently she was making his future an issue between them. *So am I,* he thought stubbornly. Her note had lacked any warmth at all and it was almost like a business communication.

Presently a blue neon light pinpointed ahead in the night and Dave slowed down until he read the sign Manhattan. Pulling into the neon-lit cinder parking apron of the boxlike cinderblock building, Dave wondered if a more incongruous name could have been dreamed up for this lonely, shabby building. Then he saw Abby's beat-up convertible parked alongside three other cars.

He entered and two men at the counter on the left looked curiously at him. At the right were a string of booths, and now Dave walked toward the rear. In the third booth, her back to the rear, Abby was seated, and when Dave halted before her, she looked up. For a moment they eyed each other warily, and then Abby said, almost shyly, "Hello there."

"Hi," Dave said. He slipped into the seat opposite her, trying to interpret the reserve in her expression. "Hutch just brought out your note," he said awkwardly.

Abby nodded. "How's it going?"

"Lousy. How's it with you?"

"Lousy," Abby said. They simply looked at each other and neither made a move, and Dave thought, *If that's the way she wants it, that's the way she'll get it.* Almost coldly he said, "Where'd you swipe the Tri-State stationery?"

"I'm Mrs. Heath's personal secretary," Abby said bluntly.

Dave only stared at her, trying to make sense of her words. "Personal secretary?" he echoed, and then added, "Since when?" in a voice of skepticism.

"Since yesterday."

Again they fell silent. Dave wanted to ask a dozen questions, but Abby's chill reserve stopped him.

"Aren't you curious about why I asked you to come here?"

"Of course. I'm curious about why you're working for her. I'm curious about how you got the job. I'm curious about why you're in Joash."

"Just say I wanted a change of scenery," Abby said coldly. "I got a job because there was one open. I came to Joash because I wondered what that blonde had besides money. I found out. It's plenty."

"Isn't it?" Dave asked, almost belligerently.

"She's in with Rex Uranium now, I understand."

"That's right. We made a deal."

Abby looked at him a long moment, and Dave stubbornly kept silent. Abby drew a deep breath now and said, "All right, here's what I came out to tell you. Watch out for her."

Dave scowled. "What do you mean by that?" he challenged.

"I don't even know myself," Abby said. "You had a fight with a man they call Chief."

Dave nodded. "Her bodyguard, yes."

"He got back from the hospital yesterday and she fired him."

"That's fine," Dave said grimly.

"Maybe you'd like to know the reason she gave for firing him."

"What is it?"

"I'll give you her exact words. She said, 'The real reason, Chief, is that I'm involved with Rex Uranium to the tune of several hundred thousand dollars. It's too important a deal to let you wreck it.' "

Dave pondered that, puzzled by it. *Several hundred thousand dollars.* Did Holly Heath figure that 10 percent of the Portland group was worth that amount? That was absurd, he knew. More than likely Holly was exaggerating in order to get rid of Chief who had caused her enough trouble.

Now Abby's voice cut in. "Is your deal that big?"

"Not possibly. She just wanted to can a nuisance. To supply a serious reason she dreamed up that story. Chief isn't connected in any way with Tri-State, so she could tell him anything and he wouldn't know the difference."

Now Abby's voice cut in, "Maybe you'd like to know why Chief thinks he was fired."

Dave only waited.

"He thinks it was punishment for fighting you because she likes you, not because of the deal."

"Malarky," Dave said promptly.

"If it's of any interest to you, I think so too," Abby said.

"It's still malarky."

Abby eyed him coldly. "How did you two get on this Dave and Holly basis?"

"Who said we were?"

"I said so," Abby said. "She refers to you in conversation as Dave because I've heard her. You must refer to her as Holly."

"All right," Dave said coldly.

Abby reached for her purse and began to move out of the booth.

"Wait a minute," Dave said. "Where're you going?"

"Back to town. I came out to tell you something I thought was important. You don't believe it, so why hang around?"

"Look, Abby," Dave said soberly. "I don't mean to sound ungrateful. You overheard something that made you suspicious, but if you understand our agreement with Tri-State it doesn't make sense." As Abby listened watchfully, Dave explained the agreement with Tri-State. "The most that is involved," he finished, "is seventy-five hundred dollars worth of drilling for Tri-State."

"I heard what I heard," Abby said stubbornly.

"You're just suspicious," Dave said accusingly.

Now Abby stood up. "All right, I am." She looked down at Dave, and her lower lip was quivering. "I came to see you for old times' sake, I guess — that, and to tell you I acted like an absolute bag when I saw you last. Here I find you with stars in your eyes over that blonde. You won't believe she's anything but perfect, so I guess I'd better go." She wheeled and walked toward the door.

Dave came out of the booth and followed her. Out on the parking apron he took her arm, and she halted. "Look, Abby," Dave said grimly, "I'm grateful for your coming out. I really am. I'm just sorry I can't buy your story."

Abby looked at him a long moment. "I don't think you're sorry at all," she said. She moved away from him, slipped behind the wheel and drove off.

Helplessly, Dave watched her, cursing under his breath. He was angry now and engulfed by a feeling of utter futility. Abby's demand that the price of their making up be the sharing of her suspicion of Holly Heath was too high a price to pay, Dave thought angrily. Only then came the dismal realization that the gulf between him and Abby was so wide that it probably could never be bridged.

The Chief never reached Salt Lake City. At Red River, a small town a hundred miles north of Joash he demanded of Perez that he be set down. Since the Chief, crippled as he was, weighed a good hundred pounds more than Perez, the polite little Filipino accommodated him. Besides, through long association in working for Mrs. Heath, they liked each other.

"What you do now, Chief?" Perez asked as he deposited Buford at a curb in the business district.

121

"I don't know, kid, but you take care of the doll now, hear?"

Perez nodded, and they shook hands. Then Chief picked up his bag and walked away. At the first beer joint he found, he deposited his bag, ordered a beer, asked the bartender for the name of a motel, called and got a room and then came back to his seat.

The beer was cool and relaxing, and only now did Chief let himself contemplate the future. There was no place in it, he knew, for going it alone. Far from being angry with Mrs. Heath for his summary firing, he felt sorry for her. She'd let him go in a fit of temper, not meaning it. He'd goofed when he thought he could haze Borthen, having no idea that Mrs. Heath valued her relations with him. He thought of Borthen a moment with purest hatred. He should have shot him, and would if he again had the opportunity. *I'll have it,* he thought cynically. As for the hassle Sunday, anybody could make mistakes, he thought solemnly; the point was he must make up for his. In doing so he must prove to Mrs. Heath that she needed him and could not do without him.

He lifted his arm tentatively and felt only small pain, and decided he could do without the sling which he lifted over his head and stuffed into his pocket. The nose bandage, of course, would have to remain.

He felt better now, a whole man. Then he ordered another beer, his thoughts again returning to the immediate problem. In some way, somehow, he must square himself with Holly Heath and get back on her payroll. *Well, I might as well start,* he thought. Finishing his beer, he asked the bartender the name of a good used-car lot and was directed three blocks south. In less than half an hour he had purchased a nondescript used car with part of his severance pay. His next stop was at the telephone office where he called the tourist court in Joash that he had left only a few hours ago.

He inquired for his old room for tomorrow night, got it, and hung up. Afterwards he picked up his bag at the bar, drove to his motel room and, feeling tired, lay down. It was noon next day before he awakened.

Unconcerned as any animal at the passage of time, Chief went downtown, bought himself a steak dinner, checked out of his room and headed back for Joash.

The thing to do, he decided on the way, was to lay low for a couple of days, then when Mrs. Heath had cooled off, tell her the plain truth, that there was no other life for him except the one he'd been fired from.

He arrived in Joash at suppertime, re-established himself in his old room and bought a solitary dinner at a restaurant where he was least likely to meet any of the Tri-State crew. After supper, perhaps out of nostalgia, he got in his new car and drove around for a look at the Tri-State lot. Pulling up on the street, he parked in front of the lot, then pulled out a cigar and lighted it. Mrs. Heath's convertible was parked alongside another convertible which he did not recognize. He watched the office trailer for a while, smoking contentedly, wondering if Mrs. Heath were still working, wondering, too, if conceivably she was missing him as much as he was missing her. Without her presence, he knew, he was just another ageing cop who, with any luck, could talk his way into the detective force in a two-bit city. With her, he was a king, demanding homage of all who would see her, eating as high on the hog as any man had a right to expect, and nourished in spirit by her prestige.

The office trailer opened and a girl stepped out and moved over to the third trailer. Chief remembered her now from yesterday, a new girl who had been typing when he went in to see Mrs. Heath. Then the strange convertible must be hers.

Years of police work had ground into Chief the habit of curiosity and observation, and now, almost automatically, Chief looked at the license plate on her car. It was a Colorado plate whose first two numbers were forty-one, designating, Chief knew, the number of the county of origin.

For a moment Chief stared at the plate. The county number was somehow familiar to him, and he wondered if he had remembered it from yesterday. Then he knew that was not possible since he had not even noticed the car yesterday. Then the clear memory came, and with it conviction; forty-one was the county number on the plate of the newest jeep that Rex Uranium drove onto the Portland group Sunday afternoon before the fight.

For a moment Chief considered the implication.

Borthen, someone had said, was from Colorado. Here was another car from the same county and its owner was working for Mrs. Heath.

Question: Did Mrs. Heath know this? Question: Was it just coincidence or was it significant? With the answer to these two questions Chief knew he would have what he was after — a way back into Mrs. Heath's good graces.

Patiently then, he waited, thinking about this, watching the trailers. As it grew dusk the same black-haired girl came out of the trailer and headed for her car.

Chief started his car, drove away and pulled around the intersection in the twilight, then stopped. The convertible came out of the lot, turned right, and Chief, his lights still off, pulled in a block behind it. As soon as the convertible turned left on the highway, Chief turned on his lights and followed.

There were no important turn-offs, Chief knew, for at least ten miles, so he dropped back to where he could only barely keep the tail light in sight. Thirty miles farther on, still tailing the convertible, he saw it pull into a roadhouse. As he passed, the girl was just entering the door of the place whose sign proclaimed it to be the Manhattan.

Chief drove on another mile, turned around and pulled into the Manhattan's parking apron next to the convertible. If this dame was the only customer, he'd be a fool to walk in, since she had heard him fired. He sat in his car and presently two other cars, almost at the same time, pulled in and parked to the left of him. A single man got out of each and went into the Manhattan. Still risky, Chief thought, and called upon his patience.

In less than half an hour Chief was rewarded. A jeep drove up and parked next to the convertible, and now, in the darkness, Chief lay down on the seat. He heard the crunch of gravel swell and diminish, and then he sat upright. It was Borthen just entering the roadhouse. For the first time in two days Chief smiled, and when he started his car to back out, he was laughing softly.

Breakfast was finished at bare daylight next morning, and Wallen waited until Dave rose and carried his plate to the dishpan. Wallen followed him, dumping his own dishes, and then said, "Can I see you a minute, Dave?"

Dave walked out of earshot of Hutch and the two miners. Then Bates said, "I got some bad news in the mail yesterday. My dad has had a heart attack."

"I'm sorry to hear that," Dave said soberly. "Is it serious?"

"That's what I don't know and what I want to find out. Would you mind if I drove into town and called home this morning?"

"Go ahead," Dave said promptly. "Like I said, if our first round doesn't turn up something good, we'll quit for the day, anyway."

"Thanks, Dave," Wallen said. "I'll be back as soon as I get my call through."

Wallen walked over to the jeep, his face sober.

Once he had wheeled the jeep out of the camp, a faint smile of satisfaction came to his broad face. As always, Borthen was gullible in all things. The fiction of his father's heart attack was swallowed whole. Now, with a full half-day free, he could settle a few things with Mrs. Heath.

Swinging past the drill camp, he saw the drill crews taking off in their jeeps for the day's work. Everson, he noted, was not about, but that didn't matter. Everything had been arranged last night.

First, when he had come to Everson after supper with the news that Dave was determined to move if better ore were not found today, Everson had told him of his previous meeting with Dave. When Wallen learned that Dave had asked Everson to direct them to a new mine location, Bates had felt both anger and apprehension. Mrs. Heath had directed him to steer Dave to the worst prospect, and Wallen had obliged. Now Dave was in almost open revolt. Worse, he was becoming suspicious of both Wallen's ability and even loyalty. Bates knew that it would take just one good argument and he would get his walking papers.

While this did not concern him much, he knew that his usefulness to Mrs. Heath would end if Dave fired him, and before that happened Wallen wanted to know precisely just how useful he was. His ignorance on that score bothered him.

To Everson last night he had insisted upon an immediate interview with Mrs. Heath, and obligingly Everson had got on the radio. Mrs. Heath, it turned out, would be all day at Tri-State's Uranium mine, and she consented to the date. As for Everson's doing the geology for Rex Uranium, it was settled between them that Everson would select the location where Bates had picked up the samples that assayed next to the lowest.

When once he reached the paved highway, Wallen turned south and in another ten miles picked up the broad gravel highway leading to the Tri-State mine.

The road climbed steadily and the canyon walls pinched closer. Presently through the haze of red dust, Bates saw the head frame of Tri-State's mine.

He drove past the tunnel mouth, envying the ore stockpile, pulled ahead past the bunkhouse and equipment park, and presently pulled into the bulldozed parking area, skirting the new metal building which housed Tri-State's office.

As he switched off the key, he mentally reviewed what he was going to say to Mrs. Heath. He wasn't sure she'd like it, but he had to know. Stepping into the office, Wallen saw a bare room holding two drafting tables. A young man in shirt sleeves, leaning over one of them, straightened up, looked around and then came over to him.

"I had an appointment with Mrs. Heath," Wallen said pompously.

"What was the name?" the young man asked.

"Never mind that. She'll know."

The young man headed for a door in the wall. Wallen saw him knock, and then enter. Presently he appeared and said, "This way, please."

Wallen followed him into a bare map-walled office containing filing cabinets and a steel desk behind which sat an elderly man in shirt sleeves. Beside him, in the only comfortable chair in the room, sat Mrs. Heath, and to her right a pretty black-haired stenographer with pencil and dictation pad in hand.

Mrs. Heath nodded her greeting and then said to the elderly man, "Joe, can you give us a few minutes alone?"

The elderly man, the mine superintendent, stood up, nodding curtly, and then the stenographer asked, "You want me, Mrs. Heath?"

"Go walk around, Abby. Maybe Joe can talk the cook out of a cup of coffee for you."

Wallen remained silent as the super and the stenographer filed out, closing the door behind them. Mrs. Heath, watching him, crossed her legs and said quietly, "You must have thought this important."

Bates came forward and settled his heavy frame into the stenographer's straight chair after first turning it so he could rest his arm on the back. Flipping his hat on the desk, he said soberly, "I did, Mrs. Heath."

Mrs. Heath waited silently while Wallen, now faintly embarrassed by his indifferent reception, tried to marshal his thoughts.

"We've got a rebel on our hands, Mrs. Heath."
"Dave?"

Bates nodded. "He's shooting off one round this morning. If he doesn't turn up better ore, he's moving."

"Show him something just as bad."

"That's the trouble, he's gone over my head to Everson. He wants Everson to pick the next spot to mine."

"Scott will take care of that."

"He already has," Bates said, and explained the arrangement between Everson and himself.

Mrs. Heath only nodded, watching him with those eyes which he was sure were sometimes warm, but which he had never seen anything but cold. Again he tried to organize his thoughts, looking beyond Mrs. Heath now so that her blonde loveliness would not disturb him. "I'm stretching things pretty thin, Mrs. Heath. I think Dave hates my guts, without knowing why."

"You mean he suspects you?"

"A little, I think. If we don't turn up decent ore at this next location, something's got to give."

"That will be Everson's fault," Mrs. Heath pointed out.

"Still, something's got to give," Bates said, and he added, "It'll be me."

"What is it you want?" Mrs. Heath asked abruptly.

This was more like it, Bates thought, and said bluntly, "I don't know what you're doing, Mrs. Heath. All I know is that you're helping him with his development work with one hand, and with the other you're having me tell him to mine worthless ore." He spread his hands and shrugged. "What's it all about?"

"Why do you have to know?"

Wallen flushed. "Mrs. Heath, I'm not under

contract to you. I've done you favors and you've been very generous. If I'm to be on your payroll, tell me so. If I'm not and this is just another favor, then tell me that." He smiled unpleasantly. "If I'm to salute and jump off a cliff with no questions asked, I'd like to do it on salary. But if I'm working myself out of a soft job as a favor to you, I'd like to know why I'm doing it."

The faintest of smiles touched Mrs. Heath's face. "I've treated you very shabbily, Mr. Wallen," she acknowledged in a pleasant voice. "I assumed our relations would remain cordial as long as there was money involved."

Wallen felt his face go hot. This woman had a talent for the veiled insult and for a corrosive politeness. Nevertheless Wallen held his temper.

"Mr. Wallen, let's say that I'm employing you for a minimum of five hundred dollars per month. Any favors you do me will be suitably rewarded."

"And I accept, Mrs. Heath," Wallen said almost sullenly, "but what is it I'm trying to do?"

Mrs. Heath seemed to Bates to be calculating, and then she said abruptly, "I'm surprised you haven't guessed."

"I guess I'm thick," Wallen conceded.

Mrs. Heath only smiled, again with malice, as if silently confirming Wallen's judgment of himself.

"It's very simple," Mrs. Heath said then. "Dave thinks the road work and drilling I'm doing for him for a 10 percent share of Portland will make

131

up most of the development work he requires."

Bates nodded.

"That lets him mine, and, he hopes, lets me pay for the rest. Your job, which you've done very well, has been to keep him mining worthless ore so he won't make money."

Again Bates nodded.

"In two weeks," Mrs. Heath continued, "I will pull out my drill rigs and destroy the road. Does that mean anything to you?"

Wallen frowned, turning this over in his mind. "Frankly, not much, Mrs. Heath. You've got an agreement with him. You've drilled for him with three rigs. There are your costs and crew time that you've already spent for him."

"Think again, Mr. Wallen," Holly Heath said quietly. "Those drills are running, but they are not drilling. The deepest hole will be less than twenty feet. I'm the one keeping costs on the drilling and road work and I'll refuse to give them to Borthen. When I pull out and destroy the road, I will have done not one penny's worth of development work — and it will be too late for him to do it."

For a stunned minute Wallen considered this. It was, he saw immediately, the blow that would sink Rex Uranium. Dave had counted his association with Tri-State as a great stroke of luck; actually it was the kiss of death, and for a brief moment Wallen felt a student's admiration for the master's hand. He said then, "Dave will sue you."

"Let him. I'll gladly pay the entire fifteen thousand required development work — after he's unable to renew his lease."

Wallen asked then, "All this is for what, Mrs. Heath? Just to make a bigger sucker out of an already big one?"

Holly Heath shook her head once in negation.

"You mean the Portland group is worth all this?"

"I'm not doing this just to flex my muscles, Mr. Wallen. While you were fake sampling the Red Ledge group, Everson was looking over the Portland group. The best ore, and more of it, lies in the Portland group. I have already put in escrow the money to purchase the Portland group from Packard. The sale is contingent upon one thing. Rex Uranium must fail either to do the development work or raise its money equivalent, so that it can't renew its lease."

Wallen whistled softly. "The full treatment," he murmured.

"That's the idea," Mrs. Heath said calmly. "Now do you see why your work is important?"

Wallen only half-heard her. He was wondering idly if he could go back and pretend to stumble upon the good ore body. He was certain he could find it in a few days, now that he knew it was here. He could get 5 percent of it under his contract with Rex Uranium.

He surprised Mrs. Heath watching him, a veiled amusement in her eyes. She said then, "In the new corporation which I will form to mine the Portland group 15 percent of the stock will go to the people who made it possible. That will mean Everson and yourself, Mr. Wallen."

Even before the pleasure came the embarrassment. She had read his mind, Wallen knew, and was now insuring against his treachery. Seven and one half percent was better than five, Wallen thought; altogether, with his share in the Portland group and his share in the Red Ledge, he no longer would have to worry about money.

He rose now and said, "That's very generous of you, Mrs. Heath."

"I think so, too," she said coldly. "Any more questions?"

"None."

"Then good day."

As Bates Wallen left the building heading for his jeep, the black-haired stenographer passed him on her way to the office. He smiled and said, "Nice day."

And passing him, she answered, "Isn't it?"

Nice day? Wallen thought. Why it was the nicest day that would ever happen in his lifetime.

5

It was full dark when Everson came into Rex's camp, clip board and map under his arm. A gasoline lantern on the rough table seemed bright as a flare in the soft night, and as Everson approached, he switched off his flashlight and squinted against the glare. Dave shoved his account book aside and Hutch looked up from the newspaper spread before him on the table.

Hutch knew there was a move in the offing. They had shot their first round at midday, and while they picked up the ore body on the new face, it was only seven inches wide. In disgust Dave had pulled off the crew, and they had spent the rest of the day readying the camp for the move.

Everson spoke to Dave and ignored Hutch who returned to his reading. He heard Everson sit down with a sigh. "Well, here's my guess," Everson said wearily, "and just remember, it's only a guess."

Hutch glanced up to see Everson unrolling the map, using the salt shaker to weigh down one end and the sugar can to weigh down the other. It seemed typical to Hutch that Everson would unroll a map before himself and not Dave; he was used to being the boss.

Dave rose, rounded the table and looked over Everson's shoulder. Watching him in the harsh light, Hutch remarked the change in Borthen. His face was leaner and, because he had seldom seen the sun in the last two weeks, he was considerably paler. Worry was riding him, Hutch knew, and that wasn't good, but he supposed that was part of youth when ambition seemed so important.

Everson said now, "Here is the rough overall geology of the group. Every numbered cross you see is where there was some radioactivity. If you follow this line of crosses you can see a fairly definite pattern running in this direction through the Shinarump." He looked up at Dave. "Since you can't drill and since you're hell bent on the mining, I suppose you'd better go in from the canyon floor here." He stabbed the map with his pencil, then consulted his clip board. "There were higher Geiger counts in this same pattern, but I don't suppose you want to bother sinking a shaft."

"No." Dave's tone was flat. "If we go in horizontally we'll pick up the better stuff eventually, won't we?"

"Eventually," Everson said dryly.

Dave straightened up. "Now where is this from where we are?"

"A couple of ridges northeast."

Dave groaned. "Can you reach it by jeep?"

"With the stuff you've got to move, a power wagon would be better."

"If we had one," Dave said wearily.

"Borrow ours."

"Much obliged," Dave said. "If you'll show me

the spot early tomorrow morning, I'll borrow it and we'll move."

Everson stood up. "That's the best I could do in the one day you gave me."

Hutch thought he detected sourness in Everson's tone.

"I'll pick you up at five-thirty," Dave said. "Again I'm obliged, Everson."

"Don't thank me yet. You may have jumped from the frying pan into the fire."

"Anyway, I jumped," Dave said gently. They bade each other good-bye and then Dave stood looking bleakly down at the map, and Hutch watched him, feeling sorry for him and liking that about him which made Hutch pity him. Stubbornness, Hutch knew, could be a curse; it could blind a man to everything else and only occasionally did it pay off. Still he admired it, since he had a large portion of it himself.

Dave's glance lifted to surprise Hutch watching him. "You heard it, Hutch."

Hutch nodded.

"You go over with me and pick up the power wagon, clean up the stuff at the tunnel first and bring the compressor on your first load. I'm going to be mining by 9 o'clock and we'll get off two rounds tomorrow if we have to work till midnight."

"All right," Hutch said mildly.

They regarded each other silently, each with his own thoughts. Quietly then, Dave asked, "What do you think, Hutch?"

Hutch cleared his throat. He was embarrassed at being consulted. "He sounds like he knows what he's talking about," he said cautiously.

"Not in this case," Dave said. "Given time, he would. I gave him one day."

"You're paying a geologist," Hutch pointed out mildly. "Why don't you follow his advice?"

"I have, and what are we in?"

"Maybe it's not here," Hutch suggested.

Dave sighed. "Is that what you really think, Hutch?" he asked soberly.

Hutch shook his head. "I just work for wages, Dave, and I've learned only one thing for damn sure since this boom." He paused so as to isolate what he was about to say. "You don't put it there by wishing."

Dave's grin was swift. *Like old times,* Hutch thought.

"You damned old pirate," Dave said affectionately. "You've got more sense than the whole pack of us." He stretched. "I'm going to bed."

Hutch watched him retreat into the tent where Wallen and the others were sleeping.

Remembering what he had heard tonight, Hutch thought, *He don't trust Wallen.* At that moment, he felt a deep sympathy for Dave. He was young and bright, stubborn, ambitious and kind. Yes, all of those things, yet his situation, it seemed to Hutch, was that of all men. Whenever fate offered you a choice, it was between two bad things, never between a good or a bad thing.

Hutch turned down the gas lamp and made it

to bed before the light died.

Next morning Hutch rode over to the drill camp with Dave and Wallen and picked up Tri-State's power wagon, a four-wheel drive truck that could almost climb a vertical wall. Driving back to the tunnel, he and the two miners hitched the compressor behind the truck, ripped up the track, loaded it and the ore car, then gathered up the hoses, water tank, jack hammer and hand tools. As they finished, Dave came from upcanyon in his jeep to guide them to the new location.

When, a half-hour later, Hutch pulled up in a wash similar to but shallower than the previous location, he looked about him. He saw Wallen upcanyon hacking at the canyon wall with his prospector's pick. With a countryman's memory for the face of the land, Hutch knew he had been here before. Stepping out of the cab, he looked about him, noting the red sandstone on the ridge to the west with the location of its sparse trees, and then the canyon itself and its far bend. Dave was coming up now, and was lighting a cigarette.

Hutch observed mildly, "Your Tri-State man wasted his time."

"How's that?" Dave said.

"Wallen sampled here. I remember it."

Dave frowned. "You're mixed up, Hutch."

"Not me," Hutch said flatly. "Ask him."

Dave turned, put his fingers in his mouth, and whistled to Wallen, and when Wallen looked up, Dave beckoned. Wallen slid down the talus and tramped back to join them.

When he halted, Dave said, "Hutch says you sampled this spot."

Wallen's glance shuttled to Hutch, and Hutch saw the swift anger and warning in it.

"Not here," Wallen said.

Hutch looked at him a long moment, and then, without a word he moved past Wallen and up the canyon a dozen yards. Then he climbed the talus of powdered gray rock for ten feet, and turned. Wallen and Dave had followed him, and now Hutch reached as high as he could, touching a spot in the gray rock. "There's where your sample came from," he said to Wallen.

For a moment Hutch thought that Wallen was going to deny it, claiming that he had prospected there in Dave's absence.

Then Wallen said, "I'll be damned. You're right, Hutch."

Hutch slid down the slope and halted beside them. Dave was watching Wallen, a frown on his face. "You mean this is one of the spots you grab-sampled?"

"I guess so," Wallen said uncomfortably.

"You knew it," Dave challenged.

Wallen's jaw was set. "All right, I did. What about it?"

"You looked at Everson's map this morning. Why didn't you say something?"

"You went over my head and asked Everson to do your geology. I would have given you my advice, but you didn't ask for it. Now he's turned up the same thing I did. Why should I bother to tell you I found it first?"

Hutch saw the anger mount in Dave's eyes, and then Dave said quietly, "I guess I bought that."

"I guess you did," Wallen said flatly.

Wallen was angry, too, Hutch saw, but it was sullen anger. Wallen said, "And now I know what you'll ask me next. Why didn't we start mining here? My answer to that is, mine it and see if you get better ore here than you did on the spot I picked."

Dave was silent a long moment, and then he said quietly, "I'll just do that."

By 2 o'clock they had shot the first round and, the sample sack loaded, Hutch took off with them for Joash. By the time he left they were already drilling the second round.

Dave had sent Wallen back to move camp and was bucking the jack hammer himself. This morning's scene with Wallen was riding him still, and he was trying to think about it calmly. Why had Wallen lied and pretended that he had not sampled this location? It could stem from professional pride and from Dave's implied doubt as to his ability, Dave knew. It was natural enough for him to keep silent, but when Hutch recognized the place, why had Wallen flatly denied he had sampled here? It was more in character for Wallen to react to the discovery with a sullen smug pride backed by an attitude of "I knew it all the time." It was Wallen's swift denial that bothered Dave.

Wallen returned from shifting camp just in time to help Dave set off the second round when it was almost dark. Afterwards they sampled and tramped back to the newly set-up camp.

When Dave saw it, he felt a small disappointment. It was on a shelf, a steep climb from the canyon floor located on too little space and backed against the red sandstone which would reflect an oven-hot heat even into the night. Still it was handy to the new tunnel, and adequate.

After a late supper, the crew turned in, but Wallen stayed up alone with Dave. It was too far now for him to walk comfortably to the drill camp; besides Wallen said he thought Hutch might bring a telegram telling him the change in his father's condition. Dave, tired as he was, made out the payroll.

It was close to 10 o'clock when they heard Hutch's jeep thrashing up the canyon. Dave knew the gas lantern would guide Hutch to the camp, and presently his lights came into sight, passed beneath them and the motor was cut. In another minute Hutch climbed up to camp. A cardboard box of small things the crew had asked him to buy for them was under one arm and a bare handful of mail in his fist.

Dave looked up from his writing and waved idly to Hutch. There would be no news on the assays, Dave knew. It occurred to him that Hutch must be weary of long drives to pack their samples to town. As Hutch approached the table, Dave made a mental note to send one of the other men in tomorrow.

Hutch handed Dave some letters and Wallen a

wrapped magazine. Wallen boredly ripped off the wrapper and leafed through a new mining journal, while Dave glanced at his mail. Suddenly he saw the familiar Tri-State letterhead on one of the envelopes. Ripping it open, he read:

Your Rex Uranium blue jeep, license No. 41-1206, drove into Tri-State Uranium mines about 11 o'clock yesterday.

The man who drove it talked with Mrs. Heath alone for almost an hour. He was a big man, probably aged thirty, wearing suntans and crepe-soled field boots. He had a wide face, blonde crewcut hair and blue eyes, and Mrs. Heath was careful not to introduce him.

Did you send him? Should he not have been there or am I still too suspicious? Abby.

For long seconds Dave stared at the letter, feeling at first only incomprehension. The Colorado license number was his. The man Abby described was undoubtedly Wallen. So, instead of driving to Joash to call his mother, he had conferred with Holly Heath. Dave thought about that a full minute, coldly weighing the implications, feeling something gather within him.

He rose now and went over to the water bag, fearful that his expression might give Wallen a hint that something had happened. It had, Dave thought, *but what is it?*

He poured out a cup of water and found his

hand shaking. He was trying to think straight now. Why had Wallen conferred with Mrs. Heath? Immediately memory went back to Wallen's refusal to stake the Red Ledge group as worthless, allowing Tri-State to slip in and stake it. Were the samples Wallen took purposely poor so that Wallen had an excuse for not staking while Holly Heath moved in?

Dave stood motionless, memory patiently backtracking. He must review everything now on the supposition that Wallen was working for Mrs. Heath. How was he to look at this present mining program?

They were mining worthless ore. Did Wallen want it to be worthless? He remembered the coincidence that Everson chose a spot to mine that Wallen had already sampled, but had denied knowing. Collusion by direction of Holly Heath?

Almost shaking with excitement now, Dave turned and walked out of the circle of lantern light to the edge of the shelf and stared out into the star-spangled desert night. *I'm being taken,* he thought with conviction. *But what are they taking me for?*

They had already taken him for the forty-four Red Ledge claims. The only thing he had left was this Portland group.

Suddenly it all came into focus. To renew his lease on the Portland group he must prove development work or pay its equivalent in cash. The only cash he could raise he had to mine. Wallen and Everson were seeing to it that he was mining nothing of value as his time ran out.

Then Abby's words, *"Mrs. Heath said, 'The real reason, Chief, is that I'm involved with Rex Uranium to the tune of several hundred thousand dollars,' "* came back to him. The Portland group then was valuable. Holly Heath knew it and wanted it. She had directed Everson and Wallen to break him.

Hands shaking, he lighted a cigarette. Now he knew his enemies. Abby, bless her, knew it all along, he thought humbly. He knew with a deep bitterness the one thing had made this swindle possible: his own ignorance of geology and mining. He had placed himself at the mercy of experts in both. He realized bleakly that he could walk past the biggest deposit of uranium ore in the world and not recognize it for what it was.

Somewhere here on the Portland group lay a fortune. In the short time left him, he must find someone with the knowledge to uncover it.

After breakfast next morning, Dave took Wallen aside.

"I've been working on the books these last two nights. We're going broke, Bates, unless there's a stock assessment."

"That's an old story to mining stockholders," Wallen said. "They've probably been expecting it."

"They'll get it," Dave said. "You take over this morning. I'm going into town and call Rex's treasurer."

Wallen nodded. "Pick up yesterday's assay, will you? I'm anxious to look at it."

You already know what it'll be, Dave thought bitterly. He turned away and tramped down the slope to the jeep.

On the way into town Dave thought over his plan. He could see no flaw in it, but he admitted wryly that just possibly there was one. He had wrong-guessed consistently for the past month, and maybe he was wrong-guessing again.

Joash was thronged as usual, but when Dave pulled in before the telephone office and went in, he saw that he would not have to wait. Night was when men were in from the field and kept the exchange jammed. He put through a call to the head of the geology department at the School of Mines, and sought a booth. When he reached him, Dave explained that his advice was wanted on the name and location of the best consulting geologist in his knowledge.

The speaker, who was also Dean of the school, admitted Dave's order was a tall one. One of the best was in Pakistan, another in Canada, and then as if suddenly remembering, he mentioned yet another, young and brilliant, who was on the Navajo reservation and who could be located through the agency there. Dave inquired bluntly about the required fee and the Dean declined any accurate knowledge, but was willing to guess that it would amount to one hundred dollars a day plus expenses.

Dave thanked him and hung up. He got through to the agency on the Navajo reservation just before noon, and was told to call back in half an hour.

When he did, he located his man whose name was Sam Prince.

Without explaining who he was, Dave asked Prince if he were available immediately, and Prince replied he had three more days' work there that he absolutely could not leave. Mentally Dave calculated; his lease ran nine more days. Counting one day for Prince's travel plus the three days he must stay on the reservation, it would leave five days for his reconnaisance. Was it enough? *It has to be enough,* Dave thought.

"If that's the quickest you can make it, it'll have to do," Dave said. "Just remember, this is urgent, Mr. Prince. The morning you get in Joash you'll find a package for you at General Delivery at the Joash Post Office. In it there will be the location and aerial and topographical maps of the group of claims you're to look over. In the same mail you'll find a five hundred dollar cashier's check for a retainer fee. When you have these you're to go" — he named a garage — "and there will be a rental jeep waiting for you. When you get on the property you'll find a drill camp. Ask them where the Rex Uranium camp is. When you reach it, ask for the lessee, Mr. Dave Borthen."

"Who am I working for?" Prince wanted to know.

"That will come out later, Mr. Prince," Dave said firmly. "You're being paid and you'll receive Mr. Borthen's permission to look over the claims. Since his permission is all you require and you've been paid, that's enough, isn't it?"

"Why the cloak-and-dagger stuff?" Prince asked.

"Very simple," Dave replied. "Rex Uranium's lease expires in nine more days. There are several parties interested in the property who wish to remain anonymous. So long as you have the present lessee's permission, it shouldn't matter to you."

"Should I wear a mask?"

"Just identify yourself to Borthen," Dave said. "That's all that's required."

"Who do I give my report to?"

"You'll be told." Dave hung up and sat in the booth a moment, undecided as to whether to make the next call. Then he knew he had to, and he asked the operator for Tri-State Exploration's number.

A girl's voice answered. "Tri-State Explorations."

"Who's speaking, please?" Dave asked.

"Miss Channon."

Dave said quietly, "I love you," and hung up. That, Dave knew, was what she wanted to know.

Chief knew he had to play this careful. If he fumbled it, all hope of getting back into Mrs. Heath's good graces was gone forever. All he had to have was fifteen minutes alone with Mrs. Heath. That, Chief knew from experience, was easier said than done. She was never alone. If he walked into the office, Mrs. Heath would order him thrown out. Besides, the nature of his business demanded privacy.

It took only a little reflection, the exercise of memory, and Chief had it. Perez was a punctual shopper, waiting until the afternoon delivery of fresh vegetables and fruits before marketing. Thus it happened that Chief was idly thumbing through magazines on the rack at the front of the market when Perez, in an immaculate white coat, came in a few minutes after three.

They saw each other at the same time, and Chief beckoned Perez over. The little Filipino had a wide smile at the sight of Chief, and when he put out his hand, Chief's great paw engulfed it.

"You come back, Chief? You hike?" Perez giggled, and Chief merely smiled benignly.

"Kid, I need help and you're my boy," Chief said, frowning as if mildly troubled. "You know Mrs. Heath fired me?"

"I know," Perez said.

"That whole gang in the office is against me," Chief went on. "I got to see Mrs. Heath alone, without any of them around."

Perez listened, his brown eyes sympathetic and alert. "You want me to bring her to you?" Perez asked.

Chief shook his head. "There's an easier way than that, kid. Just leave her trailer door unlocked and *vamos* before four o'clock."

Perez considered this somewhat dubiously. Chief could tell he was wondering what would happen to him if things went wrong.

Chief said solemnly, "All I can tell you, kid, is that she's in danger. She doesn't know it, but

I do. She's got to listen. And once she does, she'll thank you for letting me in."

"Maybe lose key, huh?" Perez suggested.

"That's right, you lost your key. I just walked in, knowing she'd come."

"Me, I don't know nothing," Perez said, giggling again. "I drive out in country to buy squab. You come, you talk, I come back with squab."

Chief laid his heavy hand on Perez' thin shoulder. "That's my boy, kid. There won't be any trouble. She'll never know you were in on it."

Perez nodded abruptly. "I buy food, leave door unlocked, go get squab."

Chief winked at him and left the store.

It had been a frustrating afternoon for Holly Heath. She had gone out to the mine yesterday with her secretary for the express purpose of drawing up a complicated mine and lease deal with a San Diego syndicate. She had gone personally rather than confer with Graham, her super, over the radio which was both noisy and, to an interested listener tuning in on the same channel, far too public. Last night, talking to her tax lawyers, she had found them unsympathetic to two of the provisions she had included. This afternoon, in spite of her yesterday's inconvenient visit, she had been required to check many of her figures by radio with Graham, and pass them on to New York. She had won her point, as she nearly always did, but it was a maddening and sloppy way to do business, and some of it was her own fault.

150

Both Joyce and Abby were typing up final copies of the lease. The radio man only a few minutes before had laid before her the monthly report from the mine. She glanced at it boredly, knowing that the work on the south slope was unchanged and that the figures would be almost identical with last month's.

Lifting her glance to the clock, she saw that it was almost four. This was tea time for her, a time when she could be alone and do for herself, with no jangling phone harassing her and with no staff to plague her with questions.

Initialing the brief report, she rose from the lounge and went out into the hot afternoon sun. Blinking against the glare, she thought that somehow if she extended this trip much longer she should find somewhere to swim. She could go up to Salt Lake, but she didn't dare leave until the business with Rex Uranium was settled.

At her trailer she put her key in the lock and noticed with annoyance that Perez had forgotten to lock the door. Stepping inside, she halted abruptly. Chief Buford, hat in hand, his face bandage not quite so immaculate as when she had last seen him, was standing beside a chair, his massive frame seeming to make the trailer a toy room. Instantly her annoyance deepened, and she asked coldly, "I thought I sent you off, Chief."

"You know better than that, Mrs. Heath," Chief said. "The only time I'll quit you is when they carry me out feet first."

151

"I meant what I said, Chief," Mrs. Heath said crisply. "There's no use begging. You're through."

Chief's big face creased in a smile. "When you hear a piece of news I've got for you, Mrs. Heath, you can hire me again, or fire me all over again. It's up to you."

"It's always been up to me."

"This'll take time, Mrs. Heath. Won't you sit down?"

Mrs. Heath did not move. "How did you get in here?"

"I had to see you alone, absolutely alone. I knew this was the only spot where you're by yourself. The door was open and I waited for you."

Mrs. Heath reluctantly accepted this; she moved over to the sofa and sat down, saying, "Aren't you making yourself sound a little too important, Chief?"

"No, ma'am," Chief said sturdily. He hesitated a moment and then said, "What would you do, Mrs. Heath, if you knew you had a spy in your organization?"

Mrs. Heath looked carefully at him. "You know exactly what I'd do."

"You have one," Chief said simply.

"Who?"

"The new girl. What's her name?"

"Abby Channon? Why, that's absurd!"

Stubbornly Chief launched on his story, telling of his return from Red River to Joash and of his watching the trailer office. He told of spotting the license on the old convertible and of remembering the new Rex Uranium jeep had the same Colorado county number. He went on to tell of following Abby Channon that same night down to the Manhattan roadhouse and waiting until the Rex Uranium jeep met her.

Mrs. Heath listened intently, at first thinking the story preposterous. But when Borthen was named as the man who met Abby, she sat up straighter. "You're not making this up, Chief? You couldn't be wrong?"

"Mind if I use your phone?"

"What for?" The question was sharp.

"I've got a hunch on this, and I want you to hear the truth." Without asking further permission, Chief moved over to the phone and gave the operator a number. "Sheriff?" he asked. "This is Buford. How are things with you?"

There was a moment of silence and then Chief said, "I'd like you to do me a favor if you will, Sheriff. Got a pencil handy?" As Chief waited, he fumbled a slip of paper from his coat pocket. "I got two names here," he said then, and gave Abby's and Dave's names, also the license number of the jeep and of Abby's convertible.

"Think you could call Ute City, Colorado, and check on both the license numbers and the names? You might find out all you can about these two people. The way I read it Ute City is a tank town and everybody likely knows everybody else's business. Just see if they're connected in any way." He paused. "No, just say it's a matter of a sizable check this Borthen wrote as down payment on a

153

mine lease. I'm just doing a favor to the claim owner. The girl? Well, it seems like she's offered to go on his note. You understand, they're probably all right, but an inquiry at their bank might queer the whole deal. Let me know what the charges are and call me back at 175 as soon as you can. Thanks, Sheriff." He hung up.

"How did you get next to him?" Holly Heath asked.

"We're both old cops. Besides, in this town, hard liquor isn't too easy to come by unless you bring it in. I brought it in."

"Tell me again about their meeting," Mrs. Heath ordered.

Feeling a quiet jubilance within him, Chief repeated his story. He knew that Mrs. Heath was concerned and maybe only a quarter doubtful of his story.

When he was finished, Holly Heath said not a word. She rose, went into the tiny kitchen and distractedly began to prepare her tea. Chief wanted to smoke a cigar, but he thought it unwise to appear too self-possessed and confident at this moment.

Presently, Mrs. Heath called him to ask if he would like some tea, and Chief politely declined.

The phone rang before Chief had finished speaking and he swiftly palmed up the phone. "Buford speaking." There was a pause. "That was quick work, Sheriff. What did you turn up?"

He listened a moment and then said, "Just a moment, Sheriff. I wonder if you'd repeat that to the claim owner. She's right here."

Holly Heath was already at his side. She accepted the phone from him, saying, "Yes, Sheriff."

A low rumbling voice came over the wires. "We checked on these two parties. Borthen is a salesman, works out of there and has always made good money. The girl is the daughter of a local doctor. If she goes on a note that isn't too steep, she's as good as gold. Car licenses check with the two parties. Oh, one more thing. The story is they are engaged to be married."

"Thank you," Holly Heath murmured, and hung up the phone. Slowly she turned and walked past Chief out to the kitchen, a quiet fury within her. She had been tricked and now, standing over the tiny stove with the kettle boiling furiously, she wondered what she had let slip that Abby Channon could report to Borthen. Nothing; she was absolutely sure there was nothing. Everson had been out at the drill camp most of the time, so there had been no conversations Abby could have eavesdropped on. Joyce knew nothing. Proper names in radio messages were coded, out of simple precaution, the code being known only to Graham, Everson, the operator and herself. There had been no correspondence about the Rex Uranium deal. The agreement was on company file, but it was no secret. The only possible information that the Channon girl could have passed on to Borthen was of Wallen's visit to the mine. Wallen most assuredly would have spoken to Abby or mentioned her if they had been acquainted.

No, there was no danger now; the danger, she knew grimly, lay in the future.

She poured herself a cup of tea and went back into the living room. With a start she saw that Chief, whom she had forgotten, was sitting patiently in his chair. "Well, Mrs. Heath," Chief began.

Holly Heath smiled charmingly. "You win, Chief. I guess I need you." Chief only smiled around his bandage.

"I'll tell Joyce this simply never happened. Have her cash in your plane ticket, unless you think you're apt to find Borthen irresistible."

"Don't worry about that," Chief said soberly. "It took me a little time, but I get the idea." He rose.

Holly gave him another, almost tender smile. "I'm forgiven, Chief?"

Chief seldom used profanity, but now he said gruffly, "Hell, I knew you never meant it."

But Mrs. Heath was already thinking of Abby.

In four days Dave learned the total meaning of patience. He was now wholly convinced that again he had been steered on to a worthless prospect by Wallen and Everson, but each morning he had to rise early and drive himself and his crew as if he really believed that the next round would break through into rich ore. All the time he was waiting, his every action lulling Wallen into a fool's sense of security.

On the fourth day, after the noon-hour meal, they tramped back to the tunnel. Dave had taken over the job of starting the balky compressor engine when he picked up the sound of a jeep downcanyon. As it neared, Wallen glanced up, but he did not. His T-shirt wet with sweat, he paid the approaching jeep no attention, but worked on the compressor. When he heard the jeep stop, however, he looked up, as did Wallen.

There were two men in it, and the driver was a young Navajo Indian. The other man who climbed out now could have been thirty, a small, wiry man, burnt almost black by the sun. He wore a dirty straw hat, soiled tan shirt, blue jeans and run-over boots. As he rounded the jeep, he flipped a careless wave to them.

The compressor noise leveled off and Dave knew the rest of the crew behind him was watching. "I'm looking for Borthen," the man announced.

"Right here," Dave said. He tramped over the pile of waste rock to the canyon floor, and Wallen followed on his heels. Dave hoped that their poor phone connection had clouded his voice enough so that Prince would not recognize it.

"My name's Prince," the small man said, not offering to shake hands. "Here's my card."

He extended the card which bore the name of Prince & Halsted, consulting geologists. Dave looked up. "If you're looking for customers, Mr. Prince, you're wasting your time. We have a geologist."

Prince laughed shortly. "No, I didn't have anything like that in mind." He paused. "I understand your outfit is Rex Uranium and that you're leasing this property. Is that right?"

Dave nodded, almost coldly.

"I've been paid to make a geological survey of this property and I was told to get your permission, Mr. Borthen."

Dave scowled and glanced at Bates. He was scowling, too.

"Who hired you?" Dave asked.

"They prefer to remain anonymous," Prince said. "The way they put it to me, Mr. Borthen, you're the lessee. They're not at all certain you'll exercise your option to buy or renew your lease. They want me to look at it, but only with your permission."

Wallen said abruptly, "I know you. You were on a job for Kennecot over by Hanksville, weren't you?"

The respect in Wallen's tone heartened Dave.

Prince nodded. "Earlier in the summer, yes."

Now Bates looked at Dave, almost as if asking permission and then said to Prince, "If you don't mind my saying so, somebody's got a hell of a nerve. Did Packard hire you?"

Prince shook his head. "I don't know Packard. All I know is that I was hired to look over what are recorded as the Portland group of claims, with Mr. Borthen's permission, of course."

Bates glanced at Dave. "Don't give it, Dave."

"Why not?"

"If you lease property, it's yours as long as the lease holds. There's nothing in your lease that requires you to let anybody who wants to go over it, is there?"

158

"He didn't say there was," Dave said shortly.

"Then I'd turn him down."

"But why?" Dave asked curiously.

Wallen's face was flushed with anger as he said sharply, "Why, damn it, man, if you rented a house, would you let every jerk who knocked on the door go over the joint to see if he'd like to rent it?"

"If he asked my permission like Mr. Prince has, and if it looked as if I might have to give up the house, sure I'd let him."

To Prince he said, "You see anything screwy in this request?"

Prince shrugged. "I don't see how it would change your setup, Borthen. If you have an option to buy this group either you'll buy or renew your lease. I assume you've had a geologist look over the group, haven't you?"

"Twice," Dave said dryly.

"Well, you'll never see my report, so it won't influence your decision one way or the other. The only person it would help would be men who would want it after you turned it down. Isn't that right?"

Wallen's jaw was set. "It's a matter of principle," he said angrily to Dave. "You've got certain rights and you ought to claim them."

"Malarky," Dave said shortly. He nodded to Prince. "Help yourself."

Prince looked from one to the other. "If there's a difference of opinion here, maybe I'd better get this in writing."

"Any way you want it, including tape recording," Dave said shortly.

"Just a minute." Prince went back to the jeep and pulled out a clip board, turned over to a fresh sheet of paper and began scribbling on it.

"Don't sign a damn thing!" Wallen said angrily.

Dave eyed him coldly. "Maybe you get a kick out of being a dog in the manger, Bates. I never did, myself."

"It's not that. . . ."

"Look," Dave interrupted angrily, "either we hack this, or we don't. It'll be within the next five days. If we do, this guy's report is just so much hay. If we don't, let him take a crack at it." He paused. "You afraid he'll turn up something that you and Everson couldn't?"

"Take it easy," Bates said warningly. "I spent the last eight years analyzing stuff that's been gone over before. So has Everson. My point is, you're being a sucker. Why, you haven't even consulted with Tri-State, who's got an interest in this group."

Dave tapped his chest with his forefinger. "I'm the lessee, not Tri-State. Either I make the grade in five more days or I don't. What happens after that, I don't care."

He looked at Wallen, wondering if the pleasure he was getting out of this showed in his eyes.

Prince came up to him and extended the clip board. "It's a very simple agreement, Mr. Borthen. It says that you give the firm of consulting geologists, Prince and Halsted, the right to survey the Portland group, of which you are the lessee."

Dave read it, took the extended pencil and was about to sign when Wallen said, "Don't do it, Dave, don't do it. You'll regret it all your life!"

Dave looked at him coldly, "Just how?"

"Take my word for it, you will."

"I've taken your word all down the line, Bates, but not now." He signed the agreement and handed the clip board back.

Prince said to Wallen, "You want to witness this?"

"I'll have nothing to do with it," Bates said shortly.

Dave turned and called, "Hutch, come here."

Hutch slid down the slope and halted beside Dave who reached for the clip board. "You're a witness, Hutch. Want to sign this?"

Laboriously Hutch read the agreement and then wordlessly put his signature alongside Dave's.

Dave handed the clip board back to Prince who said, "Thanks, Mr. Borthen. We won't be in your way."

Dave watched them drive off up the canyon, and then glanced at his watch. It was past noon, and he turned and called, "Okay, let's knock it off."

Only then did he look at Wallen and saw Bates regarding him in sullen fury.

That evening after work Bates, as Dave expected, took off after supper to visit the drill camp. Was it to pass on the news of Prince's coming?

Next morning Dave announced at breakfast

that he was taking in the samples this time, and instructed Wallen to start the new round. As for the samples, he didn't give a hang about them, but he had to see Abby. His phone call wasn't enough. In some way, he must make up to her for his disbelief in her. Every time he thought of their last meeting, a deep shame touched him. Rejected by him, still suspicious of Holly Heath, she had stubbornly assembled all the evidence to open his eyes. He could call her in town, or better yet, meet her and apologize for his blindness and pig-headedness.

Once alone in the jeep, he headed downcanyon, slogged over the two ridges, passed his old camp and pulled up at Tri-State's drill camp. Its continued presence here baffled him, making him wonder if he was wrong about Bates and Everson, and about Holly Heath wanting the Portland group. Why was she still throwing money into drilling that would count on his development work while she was steering him onto the lowest grade ore her geologist could find? Why should she help him with one hand and stop him with the other?

The first two drill crews were gone and a third was just loading aboard a jeep when Dave called, "How far down are you?"

The two of them looked at a third who must have been head driller. "Four sixty," the man said.

"How's it look?"

"We got a little kick on the jigger yesterday, but we're through it."

"What about the other two rigs?"

162

"Six hundred and nothing," the man said.

Dave waved and drove on. Roughly computing the footage drilled, Dave knew Holly Heath had put several thousand dollars into this drilling. *Why, damn it, why?* Dave thought in exasperation.

In Joash Dave decided to leave the assay before he called Abby. He turned left on the side street before he reached the business district and pulled up in front of a private home. A sign hung from the porch and bore the legend, J. Archer, Assays. Dave tramped down a gravel driveway to a large addition which had been built on the rear of the house. Entering a half-glassed door, he was immediately in a room that smelled of chemicals. In its center was a large furnace, bricked almost to the ceiling. Two long metal-covered tables on either side of the furnace held a jumble of retorts, flasks, stands, test-tube racks, stained cupels and a hot plate with wooden hood. To the left of the door was a seven-foot wooden table containing sample tins, and at the far table, wearing an acid-stained rubber apron, was Archer. He was a fat, middle-sized man, whose hound-dog jowls contrasted with his deep-set merry eyes which, even though cheerful, were dull from lack of sleep. He left what he was doing and came over to Dave, saying, "It's you people again."

Dave hefted his sample sack to a corner of the table, and Archer, scrubbing his face wearily with the palm of his hand, said, "I'll get it out by tomorrow noon."

Dave nodded, waiting, and when Archer turned

163

to go back to his work, Dave said, "How about the last assay?"

Archer halted. "Didn't they tell you?"

"Who?"

"The Tri-State people. They said they were heading out to the camp this afternoon."

"They must have forgotten," Dave said. He thought bitterly, *They know my assays even before I do.* Mrs. Heath never missed a trick. Through two geologists she had kept him mining useless ore and then herself checked to make sure it was worthless. It didn't matter but the thought of it infuriated Dave. Even Archer, who probably thought he was helping, unconsciously conspired against him.

Archer went over to his desk in the corner, pulled out a card file, leafed through it, drew out a paper and handed it to Dave.

Dave glanced at it and saw it was slightly worse than yesterday. Pocketing it, he said, "See you tomorrow," and tramped out. Rounding the house, he saw a Tri-State jeep pulled up in front of his and sitting behind the wheel was Chief Buford. Dave cut over toward his jeep and Buford watched him with a kind of still-faced amusement before he called, "Mrs. Heath wants to see you, Jack."

Dave halted, and all the old anger returned. Slowly he walked over to Buford's jeep, circled the front end and came up to him. He said thinly, "Jellybelly, from here on in you can call me mister."

He waited, seeing the hatred in Chief's pale eyes,

seeing Chief remember.

Then Chief smiled. "Mr. Borthen, Mrs. Heath would like to see you, if it's convenient."

"That's better," Dave said thinly. "It's convenient right now."

6

The drive to the Tri-State office was only a few blocks, and as Dave followed Buford's jeep he wondered what was coming. More than likely it had to do with Prince, but of immediate concern was the fact that he would be seeing Abby in Mrs. Heath's presence. *What of it?* he thought angrily. The string was almost played out anyway.

Dave pulled up beside Chief's jeep where Chief was waiting for him. Wordlessly they headed for the office trailer, Chief ahead. Chief opened the door, stepped aside, bowed in heavy humor, and said, "After you, Mr. Borthen."

Dave stepped into the trailer. Mrs. Heath was sitting at the red lounge, reading a legal manuscript. Abby was working at the far typewriter, oblivious to his entrance. Mrs. Heath put down her paper, gave him a wintry smile, and said, "Sit down, please," and when Dave was seated, continued, "We have some serious business, Dave. Just so there won't be any misunderstanding, I think we'd better have my secretary take down our conversation." She pushed a button in the wall.

Dave heard the buzzer, and his glance shuttled to Abby. She rose, picked up her book and stepped into the aisle. Only then did she see Dave. For one instant of shock Abby betrayed her surprise, and then her face smoothed over as she came up to the desk, and now Dave glanced at Holly Heath. She was watching closely as she said, "This is my secretary, Miss Channon."

Dave stood up, smiling, and kissed Abby, and then said, "Hi, Abby!"

Now Dave's glance shuttled to Holly Heath. Her face was white with anger, making her lipstick too garish and almost ugly. Dave knew then that Holly Heath had somehow learned about him and Abby, and had planned to trip them. He had cut the ground out from under her.

Now he looked at Abby and saw the humor welling in her eyes. Looking down at Holly Heath, she was more poised than her employer.

"Do you always greet secretaries this way?" Holly asked coldly.

"Only the ones I'm engaged to."

Holly Heath had control of herself now. Her eyebrows lifted in mock surprise. "How long has this been going on?"

"A couple of years, minus time out for fights," Abby said.

"Why didn't you tell me?"

"You never asked me."

To Dave Holly Heath said, "I suppose this was your idea."

Dave purposely misunderstood her. "To become engaged? Yes, it was definitely my idea."

"I meant placing Abby in Tri-State."

"I can answer that," Abby said flatly. "Dave

didn't know it until I'd been working here a while. It was my idea."

"Why?"

"Why not?" Abby countered. "You were listed as wanting secretarial help and I wanted a job."

"So were other companies."

"I never worked for a woman," Abby said mildly. "I wanted to see what it was like."

"Do you like it?" Holly asked acidly.

"When I don't, I'll quit." Abby's voice was curt.

Holly Heath leaned back. "All right, Abby, you can go."

Abby smiled at Dave and went back to her desk, and now Dave sat down and held his silence. He had been summoned by the queen and the burden of talk was upon her. She took out a cigarette now, but before Dave could get out his lighter, she had used her own; in a way it was a tip-off as to what was probably coming, Dave thought.

"Dave," she began, "I understand you've let a geologist onto the Portland group — an outsider who won't tell who he's working for."

"Where'd you hear that?" Dave asked mildly.

"It's true, isn't it?"

Dave nodded, and observed, "How news travels!"

Holly Heath preferred to ignore that; she asked, "Why did you do it?"

"What's the harm?"

"I'd guess plenty," Holly said.

Dave scowled. "Look, we've only got four days to find good ore before our lease is up. I've got to hit high grade to make it, and I will. Either I do it or I don't. If I do it, all the work this guy will do is wasted. If I don't, what difference does it make who gets it? Why do you say it makes plenty of difference?"

Holly Heath leaned forward. "Because I think somebody knows something we don't about the Portland group."

Dave only stared at her candid dark eyes and he thought, *The Borgia gal must have looked like you, chum.* Then he shrugged. "Maybe. Wallen looked at it and so did your Everson. That's good enough for me."

"But not for me," Holly Heath said flatly. "I'll make you a proposition, Dave."

Here it comes, Dave thought, and he waited.

"Kick that geologist off, transfer your lease to me, and I'll pay you what you have in it and pay the development work."

In other words, get that geologist out of there, Dave thought, and for the first time he felt a wild surge of hope. Here was the first solid evidence that Holly Heath desperately wanted the Portland group. And if she wanted it, the ore was there. Dave pretended to consider this, and then shook his head. He could play this in one of many ways, so he made his choice of playing it dumb and obstinate.

"I think we're getting into high-grade ore there, and I think I'll hit it."

"In four days?"

Dave nodded.

169

"Your last assay was five hundredths."

"I'll hit it," Dave said smugly. "We're just on the fringe of good stuff."

"But you don't know that," Holly Heath said in exasperation.

"I've got a hunch," Dave said, more smug than ever.

Holly Heath looked at him as if he were an idiot. She could not argue further, Dave knew, lest she betray her treachery.

With no attempt to disguise her contempt, Holly said, "Stop being a fool and be practical. You're in lousy ore which could get even lousier. You've got four days to clear several thousand dollars in ore that isn't even meeting your payroll. I'm offering you the chance to bail out and break even. I'm an idiot to do it, but you're more of an idiot to refuse it."

"But I tell you I'm going to hit good ore. I just feel it," Dave said with all the earnestness he could muster.

Holly Heath threw up her hands in a sudden angry gesture that startled Dave. Then she looked at him with a quiet malevolence. "What do you want for that lease?"

Here we go, Dave thought, and said slowly, "I think you once rated its value at several hundred thousand dollars."

Holly Heath looked searchingly at him, her lips parted, her eyes hard as stone. She waited a long moment before she said, "Did I? When?"

Dave smiled faintly. "Try and remember."

Holly Heath snubbed out her cigarette and said matter-of-factly, "My friend, I'm breaking my agreement with Rex Uranium today."

"You can't."

"Can't I? By 4 o'clock I'll have my camp moved and my rigs pulled off, and where will you be?"

"You've already done several thousand dollars' worth of drilling," Dave pointed out.

"Check that, will you?" Holly Heath said acidly. "Those drills have never been down more than twenty feet. Those cores were trucked in there to deceive you. I will bulldoze my road out of existence. I have not even kept cost on the work done and neither have you. Now try and prove to Packard that I've put in one cent toward your development work, will you?"

Here it was all spelled out for him, Dave thought. The last piece of a puzzle was now in place.

Dave stood up. "Mrs. Heath, I think I've got the picture," he said then. "Somehow you learned those claims are valuable and you want them. I didn't know they were valuable, but I had the lease. You offered to drill so I would think you were doing the lion's share of my development work, while I tried to find pay ore to make up the rest of the work. But now a new geologist comes in and you're spooked. You're afraid he'll discover what you already know, but what I don't. So now you yank the rug out from under me so I can't possibly complete my development work and renew my lease." He paused. "You overlooked one thing."

Holly Heath said quietly, "I doubt it."

"This new geologist is my geologist."

The color drained out of Holly Heath's face, and she simply stared at him. Dave leaned over, put both hands on the table and smiled at her. "You're beautiful, doll, but you're also dumb."

Holly Heath slapped him across the face. Dave, still smiling, straightened up and tramped back to Abby, who had ceased typing. "Come on, kid, I've just lost your job for you."

Abby looked at him blandly and then said in mock horror, "Oh, Dave, think of the children."

Dave laughed, and Abby hooted with laughter as if released from some terrible tension. Now she stood up, her old self, gathered up her purse and said to the surprised Joyce, "Get set for a brain-washing, chum. You've been sitting too close to me. Good-bye."

Dave started toward the door, and then remembered something. He went back to the radio alcove, yanked the operator out of his chair and then pulled the whole stack of radio equipment onto the floor in a metallic crash. Shouldering the surprised radio operator out of the way, he took Abby by the hand and headed for the door. Mrs. Heath was standing by the lounge, and Dave passed her without looking at her. He felt Abby tug him to a stop, and when he turned, Abby was facing Mrs. Heath.

"Mrs. Heath," she said, "you want to be a man

so damn badly, have you ever thought of shaving twice a day?"

Dave yanked Abby's arm and docilely she followed him out into the sunlight where he halted, folded her to him and kissed her. "Want to start kicking me?" he asked.

"I like this better," Abby said contentedly.

"You may not know it, but you've got a man for life."

"I'd better have," Abby said.

"You heard what went on in there?"

"Everything."

"Then you'll know why I can't take any more time, Abby, I've got to get back to camp."

"All right, but you've lost me a home, too." She nodded to the trailer. "That's where I live."

"Can't you move yourself?"

"Right now."

"But I haven't got time to move you, Abby! Why do you think I pulled that radio down? They'll be on Prince's neck as soon as they can find him. She couldn't get me to pull him off, so she'll do it herself. I've got to get out there and you've got to move yourself."

"Just wait five minutes," Abby said quietly.

"But I've got to get to the claims," Dave said in exasperation.

"So have I," Abby said flatly. "I don't know what's going to happen, but whatever it is, it'll happen while I'm with you." She turned and headed for her trailer, calling, "Just five minutes, Dave."

Dave thought of the primitive, almost animal existence he had been living and tried to imagine Abby living it. Then he laughed, Abby was right. They were no good apart and whatever happened to them should happen to them together. He got his jeep and pulled over to Abby's trailer. When she appeared in the doorway with her luggage, she was dressed in Levis, red-checked shirt and tennis shoes, and a white tennis cap was perched jauntily on her black hair. She climbed into her convertible and Dave followed her to a garage where she stored her car.

Once on the road, Dave filled in the story for Abby; he explained how the news of Wallen's visit had made him suspect that Holly Heath, Wallen and Everson were ganging up on him and of how he had hired Prince to make a geological reconnaissance. Somewhere on the Portland group, he knew now, there was a big body of ore. He had four days in which to find it, since their development work would amount to only a few hundred dollars.

Later, nearing camp, Dave saw the yellow plane cutting lazy figure-eights to the west, and he wondered if this could be Holly Heath's way of trying to locate Prince. Even if she spotted him, she couldn't get to him before Dave did. And that fact left a little time for a necessary chore.

Pulling past the camp, he went up the canyon where the crew was working in the tunnel. The four of them were bucking the ore car up the grade to the newly laid track, and as Dave cut the switch, they achieved the top.

"You stay here," he said to Abby, and swung out of the jeep. Hutch and the two miners eyed Abby curiously. Wallen had a look of puzzlement on his broad face. Dave climbed the slope to them, walked up to Wallen and hit him in the face with a sledging blow that sent him in a rolling sprawl down the slope. It took Dave three long strides to reach him, but Wallen was on his feet, his guard up.

No words were necessary. Wallen knew immediately what this was about and he had the desperate look of a man who knew this would come sometime and was now ready to face it.

Dave took the fight to him. He accepted a wild belt on his upper arm to land a bone-shaking counter blow that brought a grunt of pain from Wallen. Wallen took a step backwards and Dave knew exultantly that the fight was in its set course; his right to the heart set Bates back another step.

Cruelly Dave slashed at his face and Wallen's guard lifted and he crouched, still backing. Moving to the left, Dave herded him toward the jeep, and Wallen, unaware of the jeep, kept retreating. When he thought it was right, Dave charged, and Wallen danced back and was suddenly brought up hard against the jeep's winch. In that moment of surprise and dismay, Dave reached him, slugging vicious alternate blows at Wallen's face and midriff. Wallen rolled sideways, trying to round the front of the jeep, and Dave drove a savage blow into his exposed side.

Wallen cried out, fell to one knee, and then began to run for the slope. Surprised, Dave hesitated a moment, and then took after him. Only then did he see that Wallen was running for a pick lying against the slope, and now he made it, reached down and picked it up, at the same time whirling to face Dave.

Dave halted. Now Bates said in a voice shrill with fear, "Hit me again and I'll kill you!"

Hutch, on the bank above, did not hesitate a second; he dived soundlessly, his arms held stiffly in front of him and he hit Wallen with both hands squarely in the middle of the back. Wallen pitched forward on his face as if propelled from a gun. Dave took two swift steps, put his foot on the pick handle which Wallen still clutched. For one desperate second Wallen, kneeling at Dave's feet, tried to wrench the pick loose; Dave stamped on his hand, and then Wallen accepted defeat. He rose, fear and panic and hate in his face, as Dave's blow brushed through his guard and found his jaw and spun him half around.

Before Wallen could fully face him, Dave moved in for the kill. Rage had supplanted all caution in him now, and he slugged savagely at Wallen's face and body. Whimpering, trying to protect himself, not even fighting, Wallen back-pedaled past Hutch who was on his knees now, and into the slope.

Here he tripped, sat down, rolled over on his side, covered his face and lay motionless, sobbing.

Standing above him, Dave felt his anger drain

away, and contempt replaced it. He waited a moment until he had breath enough to speak, and then toed Wallen in the thigh. "Get up," he ordered.

Wallen heaved himself to his feet. His face was both bloody and tear-stained and his head was hung and his guard half up as if he were expecting a further whipping.

"Look at me, Bates," Dave ordered.

Wallen lifted his face and there was no hate in his eyes now, only fear.

"I know you've been working for Mrs. Heath," Dave said slowly, "I want to know one thing from you. You know where the stuff is?"

Wallen shook his head violently. "No, no!" he cried hoarsely. "You've got to believe me, Dave. I don't! I know it's here, but I don't know where. I never prospected the claims. I took just enough samples to satisfy you. You can kill me, but so help me God, that's the truth!"

Dave believed him. He glanced at Hutch and saw the grim hatred in Hutch's face.

Dave said wearily, "You're not worth stepping on, Bates. Get out."

While Hutch, the two miners, Dave and Abby watched, Bates, head hung, tramped down the wash.

Afterwards Dave told the crew that, with the exception of Hutch and the cook, they would be paid off as soon as camp was broken. He put Hutch in charge with instructions to take the men back to town once the camp was cleaned up.

Wearily then he tramped back to the jeep and slipped behind the wheel. Abby, her face pale, said nothing as Dave started the motor and pulled away.

"Did that make you feel any better?" she asked presently.

"Yes." Dave glanced at her. "Did it you?"

"I should be ashamed of myself, but I guess it did."

It took them a half-hour, following Prince's jeep tracks, to find the geologist's camp. It turned out to be simply a couple of bedrolls plus a Primus stove, grub box and gas lantern. Both men were absent, but Dave and Abby made some coffee and sandwiches. At dusk the two men came in, and Dave and Abby were introduced to Johnny Akeah, the Navajo who was Prince's School of Mines educated junior geologist. They had found no good ore indication yet, Prince volunteered.

Dave explained to Prince that he was his employer and he outlined the situation.

While he was talking, Hutch drove in with the camp gear and the cook, and they set up camp. When the gas lamp was lighted, Prince brought out the topographical, geological and aerial maps and weighted them down with rocks.

"Three days to go, eh, starting tomorrow?" Prince said. He looked at Johnny. "Ever find a pot of gold in three days, Johnny?"

"Not unless it was where I could trip over it."

Prince pointed to a spot on the map and said, "Knowing there's definitely something on this group changes things. We spent today working

178

toward the rough country in the northwest corner, but as long as we don't have to cover the whole area, let's look where the geology is most favorable." He made a circle on the upper right-hand corner of the aerial map. "Let's head for that area."

Dave looked at Abby. "For once," he said grimly, "I think I'm being steered toward the stuff, not away from it."

The addition of the tent plus the stove gave the camp some semblance of permanence in the dawn light. Though there was no reason for Abby to rise at this hour, she had breakfasted with them and seen them off.

Johnny went out and in a matter of minutes from camp they were entering the roughest kind of country. At full daylight a plane came over and they halted to watch it.

Prince observed, "That was the same plane that came over yesterday. That guy must have his eye on something."

Us, Dave thought, and he said, "Could be." He did not want to alarm Prince, but he did not think that Holly Heath, having reached the third day before the deadline, would give up without a fight. But what kind of fight, Dave wondered? She was the trespasser and the law was on his side. More than likely she was keeping close tab on him, curious to see if he was getting warm.

Again Johnny set off in the lead, heading roughly for the ridge. They climbed for three hours, keeping, when possible, to the boulder-strewn canyon floors. Time and again Prince put the Geiger probe on rock exposures and once or twice he got a faint count which he only noted on his pad. The red sandstone ridge began to loom ahead of them, and now the narrow canyon they were traveling was straight for a hundred yards ahead. Johnny, whose tireless walk was half-lope, half-run, was in the lead, Hutch behind him. Something on the canyon wall attracted Johnny, and he turned and halted.

It was then the shot came. Above them there was a splat, a shower of rock and then the sound of the shot.

Johnny reacted instinctively. He lunged across the canyon where a small gully afforded protection, and the three of them were on his heels. They barely made it before the second shot, a little lower, threw another spray of rock.

Once safe around the shoulder of the rock, the four men looked at each other, and Dave said softly, "Bingo." He looked at Prince. "Your work's done, my friend."

"You can say that again," Prince said, and his voice was unsteady. He cleared his throat and asked earnestly, "What the hell is this anyway?"

"I think you can quit looking," Dave said grimly. "Find where that shooting is coming from and we've got what we want."

"Who says you've got it?" Prince said.

"I do," Dave said softly. He looked at Johnny and Johnny shook his head. "Don't look at me, Borthen. I dodged enough of that stuff in the Marines."

Dave didn't answer. He was trying to think this through. Holly Heath had made the big gamble, but on the face of it it was foolish. True, the rifleman could hold them here for a day, but when darkness came they could escape. It was a simple matter to return to camp, head for town, bring the sheriff or however many deputies he needed, and find the riflemen. This would take only a day, giving them a full day in which to hunt for what the riflemen were protecting.

Head for town, Dave thought, and then he knew the rest of it. *What if I can't head for town?*

"I'm going back to camp," Dave said to Hutch. He was probably too late now, he thought bitterly.

"I'm right behind you," Hutch said. Had Hutch thought of it, too, Dave wondered?

Prince said sharply, "You're a couple of damn fools! All the uranium in the world isn't worth a bullet in your back."

"It isn't your back," Dave said. "Come along if you want." He turned and dashed down the canyon. Fifty yards away, in sight, was the bend which would afford the next protection.

He could hear Hutch slogging behind him. Suddenly sand geysered up in front of him, and he heard the shot.

He had almost achieved the bend when he heard the ricochet of a bullet off the canyon wall inches above his head. Rock particles stung the side of his face.

He was only yards from the bend when another geyser of sand mushroomed at his feet, and then he was around the bend, Hutch on his heels.

Once in the shelter of the bend, Dave didn't even halt. They cut a half-hour off the three hours required for the trip out. When they neared camp, Dave was almost running, and as the camp came in sight, Hutch drew alongside him. Circling a piñon tree they both halted at the same time.

Abby and the cook were over by the three jeeps, and now Abby, hearing them, swiveled her head. At sight of Dave she turned and hurried toward them.

One look at the jeeps told Dave the story. All the tires were flat.

As Abby approached, Dave saw that she had been crying and that her tears were of anger, not fear. "Damn him! damn him!" Abby said as she came up. "Look what he's done!"

Dave put an arm around her shoulder, turned her, and walked toward the jeep. "Who was it?"

"Wallen, and somebody else. Wallen held the gun on us while this other man hacked every tire with an axe, even the spares. Then he took something out of all the jeep engines."

Dave looked at the three useless vehicles, and he felt something close to despair. He raised the hood of the first jeep and saw they had taken the distributor arm.

"It's senseless!" Abby said vehemently. "You beat him up and he's just getting even."

"It's not senseless for them," Dave said thinly. "Someone's sitting on those claims with a rifle, Abby. They shot at us to warn us off. We've got

two and a half days to get him off. They knew
we'd head for town for the sheriff, so they've de-
stroyed our transportation." He glanced over at
Hutch. "I'm sorry, Hutch. He just faked me out.
I should have guarded the camp."

"With what?" Hutch asked grimly. "A pocket
knife?"

Dave glanced at the cook now who was watching
him with an expression of somber guilt. He smiled
to show that he held nothing against the cook,
who could not be expected to defend his camp
with a cleaver, and then he turned back to the
cold fire, half-sick with anger and helplessness.
They were afoot and sixty-five miles from town,
twenty miles from the nearest access highway
where they might spend twenty-four hours before
they could hitch a ride.

Dave's thoughts were interrupted by Abby saying, "Let's eat first, Dave."

The cook with Abby's help, threw together some
sandwiches and warmed the coffee, but Dave had
little appetite. Finishing eating, he offered Abby
a cigarette, lighted hers and his own and stared
morosely at the jeeps.

"Where are Prince and Johnny?" Abby asked.

Dave told her they were pinned down by the
rifleman and that they would probably be in long
after dark. Even knowing that there was no reason
for Prince and Johnny risking their lives to earn
a fee, he felt an unreasonable bitterness. He knew
that every minute lost now was irretrievable.

Hutch stood up and said, "Well, somebody's

got to leg it for help, Dave. I'll be going."

Dave shook his head. "You'll be too late, Hutch."

Hutch just looked at him, and said, "You going to quit?"

Dave's glance held his for a moment, and then for answer Dave said, "There's no time left, Hutch. Even if we walked in to get the sheriff and he got out tomorrow, it would take time to pry that rifleman out. It's too late."

"What's left?" Hutch demanded.

"We've got to get that rifleman."

Hutch regarded him a long moment and said, "There's not a gun in camp."

"There's something else," Dave said grimly. He rose now and tramped over to the tent where their supplies were stored. He appeared again with a small box and then cut over toward the jeep. Rummaging around in the tool box, he came up with a roll of black friction tape, then headed back for the fire. On his way he picked up a rock as big as his fist. At Abby's side, he knelt and opened the box of dynamite blasting caps and then, stripping the friction tape, he carefully taped a half dozen caps to the rock so that they were evenly spaced around the perimeter.

Rising now, he glanced off at the slope of rock lifting behind the jeeps, then wound up and hurled the rock over the jeeps.

The homemade grenade, when it struck the rock face, detonated with a sharp crack in a geyser of rock dust.

Dave looked over at Hutch.

"What's the matter with dynamite?" Hutch said.

"You can't mine uranium while you're in jail for killing a man," Dave said. He paused, still watching Hutch.

"What're we waiting for?" Hutch asked.

Calmly now, with Abby white-faced and silent, they planned the attack. They could not hope to reach the rifleman before dark, but with the aid of binoculars, they could hope to locate him today. Under cover of darkness they could move up and at daylight, if Prince or Johnny could draw his fire so that he betrayed his exact position, they would have their chance.

When they were finished, Abby shook her head. Dave asked her to fill a rucksack with food and, sick with apprehension, Abby went to work. Hutch refilled their two canteens and threw two more into the sack while Dave carefully padded the box of blasting caps and packed them in last.

Ready to go, Dave shrugged the rucksack gently over his shoulder, and Abby watched him.

"You've got to do this, I suppose," she said finally.

Dave moved over to her, tilted her chin up, and said, "I can always go back to selling asphalt tile, baby."

Abby tried to smile, and said huskily, "Get out of here, then."

Dave kissed her and headed out of camp, Hutch behind him. Wearily they backtracked and reached the bend in late afternoon. Lying on his stomach,

Dave took off his hat and crawled so that he could see around the bend. Johnny was squatted against the wall and Prince was lying down dozing, waiting for darkness.

Retreating, Dave gave Hutch his instructions. Dave was going to backtrack until he could find a way up the canyon wall. Hutch was to give him a half-hour and then attract attention of the rifleman by waving his jacket. With the binoculars, Dave would try and locate the rifleman's position.

In less than twenty minutes Dave had made his way up the steep canyon wall and, screened by a low-growing juniper, he lay on his belly and scanned the distant tree-studded ridge and the dozens of canyons that fingered down from it.

Glancing at his watch, he saw that his time was up and that by now Hutch would be trying to attract the rifleman's attention. Sure enough, within a single minute, came the sound of the first shot.

Dave could see nothing. At the sound of the second shot, however, he shifted his glasses slightly to the right, and thought he picked up the telltale smoke which had vanished before he was really sure; he held his glasses on the spot until his eyes began to distort the image. Then came the third shot, and Dave saw a brief puff of smoke. It came from a kind of peninsula of the ridge, a tangle of rock, screened by sparse trees that seemed to be growing on a stubby shelf.

Dave could not see the rifleman, but he knew he could not have been mistaken. Now he took a compass reading on the position and backed away.

On the canyon floor again, as they waited for dark, he described to Hutch the location of the rifleman and what seemed to be the best approaches. Just before full dark, the rifleman opened up again as if shooting a parting warning, and minutes later Prince and Johnny, running pell-mell, rounded the bend. Dave and Hutch had gathered enough fuel for a small fire which they had built against the canyon wall. Prince came up to them and Dave saw the boredom and anger in his face. Extending the canteen to Prince, Dave said, "Some days you can't even make a buck."

Prince grinned dryly and extended the canteen to Johnny. "Well, I've caught up on my sleep anyway."

"That's good," Dave said, "because you won't get much tonight."

Passing out Abby's sandwiches to the hungry men, he made his proposition. With any luck, he and Hutch would take care of the rifleman at first light tomorrow. If they were successful, they would summon Prince by firing three fast rounds into the air.

"With what?" Prince said.

"His rifle," Dave answered, and as Prince shook his head in doubt, Dave concluded, "In your racket you've spent plenty of nights out without a sleeping bag, Prince. Want to try it again?"

"If you two are damn fool enough to try this, it's all I can do," Prince said curtly, and added,

"You mind, Johnny?"

"Are you kidding?" Johnny asked, grinning. "I was twelve years old before I even saw a bed."

At full dark Dave and Hutch started out, and at the end of the straight canyon stretch parted company. Once Dave with the aid of the compass had given Hutch a landmark on the ridge silhouetted against the night sky, he accepted his share of the dynamite caps and tape and vanished into the night. Since Dave had selected the south side of the rifleman's ridge, he began his climb out of the canyon. It was dangerous and painstaking work even when his eyes had become fully accustomed to the dark. Yard by yard, feeling his way, Dave made his way out of the canyon, down into another, out of it and down into yet another before he turned toward the ridge. His greatest fear was of taking a fall which would detonate the caps wrapped securely in a handkerchief in his shirt pocket. Sometime after midnight well toward the ridge, he rested, ate his last sandwich, and yearned for a smoke.

Checking his bearings, he went on, climbing steeply and as quietly as he could, and well before false dawn he was in the canyon that led to the rifleman's roost. Quietly then, he moved up-canyon, clinging to the left bank, feeling the wall for a break in its expanse. Presently the wall fell away briefly for a wedge of eroded gulch and Dave knew this was as close as he probably could or should get. The next half-hour he spent in trying to climb the steep gully as noiselessly as possible.

Feeling ahead of him, he would find a secure rock, then stack behind it the stones above, which would roll noisily if he climbed over them. It was painfully slow work and after each sound he made he expected to hear the crash of gunfire from above.

When he had climbed until the gully seemed almost sheer, he moved to the right, and found a stubby piñon which would serve as an anchor.

In the last minutes before false dawn he fashioned a half-dozen blasting cap grenades and tucked them inside his shirt.

Prince's instructions were to make a distraction at first light, and now Dave waited for it, wondering what sort of shelter the rifleman had chosen and what the shape of the land was. There was no assurance, of course, that the rifleman would be in the same place today that he was yesterday, and indeed, if he were smart, he would change positions, Dave thought.

He waited, his pulse quickened, listening to all the morning sounds around him, of the earth and its creatures wakening anew.

Now, with the light dawning swiftly, he saw what he had climbed in the night and wondered how he had managed. Below the ground dropped away seemingly sheer; above him was the rimrock, and to the north and above there was yet more crumbled rimrock that closed off the view. A half-dozen stunted piñons lay upslope in the north. Still he waited.

Then from the caved rimrock to the north and above him, beyond the trees, came the near crack of a rifle. Dave lifted his face. Grenade in hand, Dave clawed his way up to the next tree, hoping that the sound of the rifle had momentarily deafened the rifleman. He was a tree closer now, looking up at the fallen red rock which jutted out toward the canyon.

Now the rifle spoke again, but less loud, and for a split second Dave wondered at the change of directions; then it occurred to him that the rifleman might have spotted Hutch.

Even as he was thinking this there came a different explosion, and Dave knew this was one of Hutch's grenades. He took his first grenade and then, in stiff-arm fashion, lifted it high toward the rimrock. Seconds later it exploded with a crash, but Dave was already in motion. He thought he heard a cry above, and now he fumbled out the second grenade, clawing his way up past the last tree and into the heap of caved rimrock.

Two more rifle shots followed in quick succession, pointed away from him. Desperately Dave looped the second grenade. He heard it crash downslope and knew that he had thrown over.

Climbing over the crest of the jagged rimrock, he was fumbling the third grenade from his shirt when he stopped suddenly. There among the jagged rocks, not twenty yards away, stood Chief, his back to him, his rifle to his shoulder, pointing it down. *At Hutch*, Dave thought, and now throwing the third grenade like a baseball at Chief's feet, he leaped off the ridge and down the short slope.

The grenade exploded at Chief's feet and at this

close range the blast was deafening. Chief lurched against the drive of the rock fragments, half-lowered his gun and turned. Too late, he saw Dave and tried to swivel his gun around. Dave hit him solidly, both hands driving for the rifle. Then Dave wheeled, yanking savagely, turning his back into Chief's body, trying to twist the gun from his hand. Dave felt the massive weight of him shift on the point of his shoulder. Then Chief was dragged off balance to his knees, but he held grimly onto the gun. Dave, still wheeling, yanked again, but Chief held on, trying to fight to his feet.

Now Dave had turned full circle, and again Chief, his back to the canyon, was still off balance and savagely straining to fully regain his feet. It was then that Dave threw a rough hipblock into Chief, at the same time throwing his whole weight into Chief's laboring body. Chief fell on the shelf edge, still clinging to the gun, and then slowly slid off. His grip on the rifle stock was broken loose by his falling weight, but he held like grim death onto the barrel with his other hand. His weight pulled Dave to his knees, but Dave held doggedly to the rifle. For perhaps three seconds they stared at each other in straining hatred, Dave kneeling, Chief hanging by one hand to the rifle barrel; then Dave felt Chief's grip slip down to the rifle sight. Now the rifle was pointed straight at Chief's head, and for a fleeting second Dave knew that if he touched the trigger, Chief was dead.

Dave could see the knowledge of this in Chief's

eyes, above the dirty bandage, and beyond that was a desperate weariness. Chief's hand slipped lower, and now Dave knew that the sight was cutting into his palm. Then in one final frantic effort, Chief raised a leg against a rock, braced himself, let go and fell.

The drop was about forty feet onto loose rock. Chief landed feet first and was immediately catapulted down by the pitch of the slope. He fell hard on the first somersault and then rolled over and over in a moil of dust and sliding rock until he hit the canyon floor. Breathlessly, Dave watched as Chief tried to get up and could not. Now Hutch, from upcanyon, ran toward him, and Dave rose wearily. He checked the shell in the chamber, then looked about him and saw Chief's meager camp gear. There was a short-wave radio on a blanket: Dave guessed Chief had been in contact with the spotter plane. Along with the remains of a sandwich were several boxes of cartridges. Now Dave slipped two more shells into the chamber and fired three quick shots, his summons to Prince. Afterwards he dropped down the slope, sliding wildly among the loose rock until he hit the canyon floor.

Hutch was kneeling by Chief, who lay on his back in the sand. As Dave came up behind Hutch, he saw that all the fight was gone out of Chief's eyes, and that he was in pain.

Hutch glanced up. "Arm's broke," he said. "Damned if I ain't glad, too."

Looking down at Chief, Dave felt no pity for

the man. It was only luck that Hutch was alive.

They made Chief comfortable and were just finishing a crude job of splinting his arm with the straightest sticks of cedar they could find when Prince and Johnny arrived. Dave explained to them what had happened and then he went over and knelt beside Buford.

"Chief, we're going to find the stuff anyway. Want to tell us?" Dave asked. "Don't think we're going to quit and hunt up a doctor for you, though. It's up to you. Tell us and we'll get you out of here in fifteen minutes. Don't and you'll wait until we've found it."

The old hatred was back in Chief's eyes. "I can wait, Jack."

Dave straightened and moved over to Prince. "He's not talking. It's all yours now, Prince."

Prince was looking up toward the rimrock to the north. He said quietly, "All right," and then added to Johnny, "Follow out this canyon, Johnny. Give me the counter."

Hutch and Johnny headed up the canyon, but now Prince started up the steep slope, Dave, rifle in hand following.

It was a laborious climb and when Dave was sure they were far enough away so that Chief could not possibly make it, he cached the rifle and went on.

Some excitement seemed to be pushing at Prince as he angled up the slope, past the tumbled rimrock where Chief had stationed himself, and above it. Now he halted, switched on the Geiger Counter and they both saw the needle jump. Moving up until they were under the towering rimrock, Prince put his probe against the yellow-brown altered zone in the gray sandstone that seemed to be inter-bedded with a thin band of mudstone.

The Geiger needle leaped upward and when Prince snapped on the speaker, there was a sustained roar of static.

Now Prince pulled out his prospector's pick and hacked out a chunk of rock and pocketed it, then began to move north.

Dave let his glance travel ahead and saw that this same band, sometimes as thick as twenty feet, stretched out far ahead of them under the rim.

Fighting for footholds, he and Prince traversed under the rimrock for an hour, Prince methodically sampling and the Geiger Counter never silent. They had traveled perhaps a thousand feet under the rimrock when the formation pinched out, and now Prince turned.

Dave could see the excitement in his eyes, but Prince said nothing. He started down the slope now and when, twenty minutes later, they hit the benched canyon floor, Prince halted.

Wordlessly he shucked off his jumper whose pockets were loaded with samples, and then reached in his hip pocket.

Dave thought he could stand it no longer, but he kept silent. Now, with his prospector's pick, Prince expertly broke the samples to the size of the rock in his hip pocket. When he was finished, he switched on the Geiger Counter and put his check sample against the probe. The Geiger dial moved far past halfway. Now, removing the Geiger Counter twenty feet away, Prince put each sample individually against the Geiger probe. Some samples kicked the needle higher than the check sample, others not quite so high, but close. When he finished the last sample, Prince, who was on his knees, looked up. "Brother!" he said softly.

"That it?" Dave asked.

Prince nodded. "In spades." He pointed back to Chief's hideout. "The underlying clay below that fifty-foot stretch of rimrock must have sloughed and the rimrock caved out, exposing this stuff. All the time I was up there I was afraid the counter was picking up a mass reaction of low-grade ore. Down here, away from the stuff though, these samples won't lie." He picked up the check sample he had originally carried in his hip pocket. "That's high grade, two percent. Some of this is higher, and I'd say all of it would average better than fifty hundredths. The ore outcrop in the channel is sometimes twenty feet thick and never less than four on its one-hundred-foot exposure." He rose, grinned and extended his hand. "You're about to be on a first name basis with the United States Treasury, Borthen."

Dave waited for the wild joy to come, but mostly what he felt behind the pleasure was a vast sense of relief. Here was the ore, but he had just one more day to meet his development work or raise its money equivalent if his lease was to be renewed.

An hour later they were back where they had

parted from Hutch and Johnny. Dave fired three shots to call them in and then went over to Chief, who was drowsing in the shade of the canyon floor. At Dave's approach, he opened his eyes. Dave knelt by him. "We got it, Chief."

Chief said nothing.

"Now listen to me," Dave said. "Wallen came into our camp while we were gone and wrecked our three jeeps. You're seventy miles from a doctor, Chief. You understand that?"

Chief only nodded.

"Then how did you get in here?" Dave asked. "A jeep?"

Chief looked at him malevolently. "Find out." He was going to play out the string, Dave knew then.

Hutch and Johnny soon came down the canyon, and Prince told them the news of the discovery. When Johnny and Hutch had looked at the samples and were talked out, Dave broke the news to them. "If Tri-State doesn't take this over, I've got to be out of here by tomorrow at midnight to renew my lease. As you know, our jeeps are wrecked. Chief won't say how he got in here, but my guess is by jeep. If we get out of here, we've got to find it."

"Other side of the ridge?" Hutch asked.

"Could be, unless he circled way east of our camp and came up from the north."

Johnny suddenly seemed interested. "What's so hard about finding it?" he asked.

"Do we beat all these canyons?" Dave asked dryly.

Johnny shook his head and grinned. "You white men don't belong in this country. Why don't you give it back to us? I'll find your jeep." Without another word he started up the slope. The others fell in behind him, mystified. They climbed past Chief's station and above it, moved along the rimrock until they found a break in it where they could climb to the ridge.

Once on the ridge, Johnny circled the spot above the break, looking at the ground for tracks. He made another circle, wider, and found what he was looking for, the print of Chief's boot. He turned and began to walk north. Moving at a tireless pace, looking only occasionally at the ground, weaving in and out among the piñon and cedar, he traveled the ridge for a half-mile. Suddenly, he cut sharp left, dropped into a steep canyon and traversed its boulder-strewn floor for perhaps a mile and a half. Not once did he hesitate. Presently, they turned a bend and there, pulled up against the canyon wall, was a Tri-State jeep. Johnny looked at them and said, "That was tough," and laughed.

The jeep, Dave noted, had a winch, and when he saw it he knew what he had to do. With a winch he could get over the ridge and to Chief who otherwise would have to lie out two more days. There was no choice.

"Just in case you're wondering how to get out of here," Johnny said dryly, "just follow his tracks."

Dave looked at his watch and saw that it was

almost four. It would cut it close, he knew, but he thought it could be done. Then he said, "Not me. We're taking this jeep up the ridge and over."

"Why?" Prince asked.

Dave said thinly, "Much as I'd like to leave Chief out here for coyote bait, I can't do it. He needs a doctor and I'd better get him to one."

It took them until evening to reach the ridge; they winched themselves up the steep grades, built roads to avoid high centers, and ballasted the jeep with their own weight to traverse steep slopes. On the ridge they drove to the break in the rim-rock, and now, in the dusk, Dave pulled out the winch cable, anchored it to a piñon and set the winch in reverse. Slowly the jeep backed down through the break, almost hung for a moment, then slowly jolted backwards down the almost sixty-degree slope, checked by its cable. Just before the cable played out, the jeep backed into a piñon.

With the other three securing it, Dave climbed back up the slope, unhooked the cable, found a stout tree below the break and anchored the cable again.

Only half the cable was expended by the time they reached the canyon floor.

It was dark when they loaded Chief into the jeep and drove down the canyon to where Prince and Johnny had waited this morning. They shared their last food with Chief and settled down in the still warm sand for another restless night.

They were moving at false dawn, and today was

a repetition of yesterday's efforts. This time, they had to be more careful because of Chief, but even so, they drove into the base camp in early afternoon.

Abby stood hesitantly, watching them as the jeep pulled up. Now Dave jumped out of the jeep, ran over to Abby and gathered her in his arms. "We got it, baby, we got it."

Abby was shaking, and now she leaned her head on Dave's chest and closed her eyes for a moment. "You great big wonderful fool," she said then.

"There's a lot to tell you, Abby, but we've got time to make," Dave said. Grabbing her by the hand, he went back to the jeep. "Chief, you stay in. Prince, you and Abby come with me. Hutch, I'll be back tomorrow with tires and distributor arms. Whiskey, too." He tramped over to the tent, threw in a jerry can of gas and, remembering Mrs. Heath's threat to destroy her road, a couple of shovels and a pick.

At the abandoned drill camp, Dave saw that Mrs. Heath had kept her promise. The gully was bulldozed clean of a road.

Through the long afternoon, bone weary and almost beat, Dave alternated with Prince at bushwhacking, at making roads and at winching their slow way toward the access road. Mrs. Heath, Dave thought grimly, had spent five times the money on destroying the road that she had spent on making it.

It was after dark when they hit the access road and headed for the highway.

Abby was sitting beside Dave, and now in the cooling evening, she said, "Can I ask something?"

"Go ahead."

"You've got a lot of uranium ore you say, but the deadline is up at midnight, Dave. What good will it do you? Your development work isn't done, and you haven't got fifteen thousand in the bank. Can you get it before midnight?"

"I'm betting I can," Dave said. *If* he could, Dave reflected, it would mean that he could renew his lease and mine enough ore to exercise his option to buy the Portland group. Within a couple of months he could haul ore out, the value of which would pay the Portland group many times over. Holly Heath, once he had exercised his option to buy, would be unable to harm him; this land would be his. Chief, if he ever trespassed upon it, could and would be jailed.

As for himself and Abby, there would be the September wedding and by that time there would be money enough in the till for them to take a wedding trip around the world if they wanted. *If I can get the money,* he thought wearily.

It was close to 9 o'clock when the blue neon lights of the Manhattan roadhouse showed ahead. Dave pulled into the parking apron, switched off the motor, pocketed the key and said, "Come along." Everybody, including Chief, followed.

A party of ranch kids noisily occupied two of the booths. Dave got some change, from the waitress, and went back to the phone in the rear. Chief sullenly chose a stool.

When Dave had the Joash operator, he said, "Connect me with Will Cushing at Cushing Minerals. I know they're closed, but find him. You know his secretary?"

"Laura Mayes? Of course I do," the operator said.

"Get her if you can't get him, and tell her to get hold of him, and quick."

"Uranium stuff?" the operator asked.

"That's right."

"Uraniums, geraniums," the operator scoffed. "All right, honey, where are you?"

Dave told her and hung up, and turned to find Abby and Prince at his shoulder.

"Let's get some coffee," Dave said, his voice barely controlled.

The three of them sat at the counter, silent. There was nothing to say and only time to kill. Abby's hand moved over and touched Dave and he looked at her with weary affection. Everything, Dave thought grimly, was now committed; it was out of his hands.

When the phone rang, Dave dropped his cup of coffee with a crash and ran for the phone, Prince and Abby behind him. The operator said, "You the party calling Mr. Cushing?" When Dave said he was, he heard Cushing's voice, "Who's this?"

"Dave Borthen, Mr. Cushing, Rex Uranium."

"Oh, yes," Cushing chuckled. "How's the big operator?"

"Right now, big," Dave said. "You want to be cut in on it?"

"Wait a minute," Cushing said slowly. "Cut in on what?"

"The Portland claims."

"That dog, why . . ."

"Just a minute," Dave said. "You know Sam Prince?"

"Very well. What about him?"

"He's right here. Talk to him, will you?"

He handed the receiver to Prince who said, "Hello, Guy!" There was a pause. "No, he's not kidding. There's close to a hundred feet of exposed channel and the ore body's from four to twenty feet thick. On a rough field assay it tests up to two percent and will average fifty hundredths and the tonnage is there." He paused again, then laughed. "This is no con, my friend. I just wish it were mine."

He handed the phone back to Dave, who said, "Satisfied, Mr. Cushing?"

"Prince's word is good enough for me. What kind of a deal you talking?"

"You got fifteen thousand dollars in the bank?" Dave asked.

Cushing laughed. "I did have. I might not have when I get through with this poker game you're interrupting."

"This is important, Mr. Cushing," Dave said. "Write out a check to Dan Packard for fifteen thousand dollars and mark it 'Rex Uranium development work on Portland group.' Can you find Packard tonight?"

"By reaching out my arm," Cushing said. "He's

in the game, too."

"It's due before midnight if I'm to hold the group."

"Can do, but first what kind of deal are you talking?"

"You write it, Mr. Cushing. It's big enough for everybody."

"Fair enough. I'll see you when?"

"Tomorrow," Dave said. Now he felt Abby's hand steal into his. Looking down, he saw her watching him happily. "One more thing, Mr. Cushing, will you make a phone call to Mrs. Heath at Tri-State?"

"Sure thing."

"They were in with us," Dave said. "Just tell her we found it. Tell her thanks for the wedding present. She'll know what I mean."